The Tree

By James Reece

Thank you for buying this book, the proceeds will go towards helping me build a memorial to the NHS.

In honour of their outstanding bravery during the 2020 Corona Virus pandemic.

Also included

Eyes of The Fox

The Rhyming tale of an accidental, but magical bond, between a boy and a wild Fox.

I hope you enjoy my stories.

James

To Mia, best wishes

James Reece

Prologue

In the heart of London town as a warm spring day dawns, it is within a small city park that my story begins.

Encircled by a ring of restless roads, and surrounded on all sides by skyscrapers reaching high into the sky.

With its thick hedged walls and tall old trees, this carefully planned oasis of green, does its best to keep these two contrasting worlds apart.

In fact, from inside the park, the illusion of being in the countryside is completely convincing. It is only the dizzying sight of looking straight up, that reminds you of where you really are.

Even though these tiny patches of nature, are scattered few and far between. They are thoroughly appreciated by all of those who find a moment or more, to spend within their walls.

This is a place that humans, birds, bees, and bugs of all kinds can enjoy. Taking temporary relief from the grey and glass that stretches in every direction, as far as the eye can see.

It is in this one particular remnant, of the lush woodlands and fields that were once all around. That a special little life is about to be born.

I should probably warn you at this moment, this is a Spiders story! And within it, there are more than a few of them!

So, if you are not too fond of Spiders, there are a few parts that may make you a little bit squeamish. But it will be worth a little discomfort to hear this tale, of the incredible journey that one of them is about to go on.

Chapter 1
A wandering mind

Deep inside the ever dark core of a thick green shrub. A young mother Spider busily wraps a soft silken blanket, around her average sized clutch of baby Spiders.

(An average clutch being 1000 Spiderlings by the way.)

She had picked the perfect spot, tucked away in a secluded corner of the park. It was dark, quiet, and very well guarded from any hungry prying eyes.

Although the beautiful flowers of this well matured Fuscia, draws a lot of attention from people, insects, and all other manner of passers-by. They are always far too distracted collecting pollen, or sniffing the sweet smelling flowers to notice the ball of silk. It hung far from view, suspended deep within the bushes densely packed branches.

She knew that there, she could safely leave them. At least for long enough to nip out to the bushes edge, where she could hunt for a well-deserved, and much needed snack.

The silken ball quickly swelled, as the babies grew within. Until one day, it finally burst open.

There gazing back up at her, were 4000 pairs of tiny little eyes.

It is a well known fact, that not many mother Spiders hang around for long after their job is done. But she was a good mother, and she protected them until they were big enough to fend for themselves.

As they scurried about finding their numerous feet, she imparted useful gems of ancient spider wisdom to them. This important information had been passed down from mother to Spiderling for many, many generations.

The lessons were mostly about which creatures were good to eat.

But also which creatures to avoid, as they thought they were good to eat.

There were also numerous demonstrations of different types of web, including where and when to use them. It turns out she was also a rather good teacher.

Now, as I'm sure you can imagine, having 1000 children in front of you, made it impossible to take any questions. Or even to ask any questions of them, the noise of all those little voices giving different answers at once, would be very confusing. And definitely not the most constructive way to use the little time that she had with them.

So it was made quite clear that anything she did say, which sounded like a question. Was unless otherwise stated, completely rhetorical.

For example. "Why do we stay hidden as much as possible? Ssssshhhhhhhhhh! So we don't get seen by a hungry bird, that is why!"

After that was clearly understood by everyone, they all sat and listened intently, in silence at last.

That is all but one, but we will come back to him!

Now choosing a name for one child is hard enough, so picking 1000 all at the same time would be an absolute nightmare.

That is why traditionally, each Spider finds their own name in due course. The name depends entirely, on the first name worthy thing that distinguishes them from the others. Unfortunately, they cannot choose a name for themselves. A spiderling can only be given their name by another.

Which as you will see, is a big part of this story.

This is the tale of one particular, very easily distracted Spiderling, who will be given his name eventually. But you will have to wait until near the end of the story, to be absolutely sure what that name is.

So for now, until he finds his name, he is simply called Spider. As are all of the other Spiderlings in the family, at this moment.

All except Trip!

Poor Trip, literally the first thing she did was get her leg horribly tangled up in the web. She tried desperately to unravel herself, only to get her other legs also caught up in a knot. this sent her flying head over heels, right in front of everyone.

Of course, the name stuck immediately. But at least, she will never be forgotten. Her 999 brothers and sisters will always remember her, even if it is for an embarrassing reason.

But now back to Spider, who wasn't paying attention to any of the important lessons being given. He was, yet again, gazing up in wonder. Fascinated by all the dots of light that travelled over his head, once every day.

At this moment however, he had absolutely no idea what they were. In fact they were just tiny gaps in the leaves above, where the sunlight managed to find a way through.

He was right in the middle of one of these daydreams, when something his mother said caught his attention. For once, he turned, and listened to her with the others.

She said, "Build your web high, and build your web strong, if you don't want to go without food for too long."

"I tell you no lie, the best food is a fly, to catch them a plenty make your web in the sky."

"The more time that you spend, on the height you ascend. The more feasts every day, you will have to attend."

This was about the only thing she had said, that Spider had given any thought too whatsoever. That, and web building, he did love building webs.

He would always make unusual patterns in his silk, most of them completely impractical for catching flies. But, they were always interesting, and always very popular with everyone else. Everyone except his mother of course, she just frowned at their impracticality.

His mother then continued, "I hope you have all been paying attention!"

Spider gulped, and thought to himself, is there going to be a test?

"The world outside this bush, is riddled with peril. But fear not, all of the things I have taught you, will help you to survive the many tests that are to come."

"One day girls, it will be you teaching these valuable lessons to your own Spiderlings, so remember them well."

"Now it is my time to leave you, I love every one of you dearly, and I wish you all good fortune!"

With that, she was gone! She swiftly slipped down to the grass below, gliding to the ground on a long strand of silk. The Spiderlings all watched in silence, as she scurried off into the distance.

Chapter 2
Split decisions

The next day, the Spiderlings all huddled nervously together. Suddenly they were all very scared at the thought of being alone, and completely unprotected.

During that night, a handful* of the braver youngsters amongst them, decided to use the cover of darkness to make a break for it. Out into the unknown wilderness beyond, they ventured.

(*Not a human's handful of course, as that would have been all of them. It was more like a mouses' paw full.)

The adventurous Spiderlings dropped to the grass in perfect formation, like an abseiling display team. Then scattering off all in different directions the second they touched the ground.

The others just watched in pure amazement, as their pioneering siblings drove out into the dark unknown. Boldly storming towards the many mysteries, and many, many dangers that lay ahead in the blackness beyond.

A mixture of strong feelings ran amok through those that remained, they jostled to be as far from the exposed edge as they could. Shuffling nervously together, into the tightest ball they could. Eventually, they settled down for the night.

As the dawn started to rise, nearly all of the Spiderlings were already quibbling about what they should do next. All the, "How do you knows," the "What about thats," and the "If only we coulds." Blended together into an incomprehensible, hypnotic hum.

Some were just stunned with their mouths agape, in awe of the unbridled bravado, shown by their fearless brothers and sisters. While others let their imaginations run wild, and just sat there, quietly shaking. They were terrified by thoughts of all the horrible potential destinies, that lay in wait for them out there.

Maybe in some ways it was good that Spider had missed most of his mothers lessons, as he did manage to pick out the words Mother said," a few times from the chatter. He had absolutely no idea what any of them were so scared of, but it was clearly a result of their mothers' teachings.

As the others carried on squabbling, Spiders' eyes drifted upwards, as they did every day when the lights appeared above. Drawn to the flickering tapestry of light that always appeared at this time. They travelled slowly but relentlessly, from one side of the bush to the other.

The lights seemed to move with such a timely rhythm, Spider felt that they must have some distinct purpose. There was also an unpredictable element to their nature, their brightness and colour would change at random moments during their journey.

Spider had a good long blink, as he always did at the stunning sight unfolding overhead. But not because the light was too bright, and he did not blink in unison as you would expect from a traditional blink.

His eyes would flicker shut, and then open again, in a rather amusing way. His blink rippled wildly across his face, as his eyes closed independently of each other. Creating almost limitless different combinations.

Spider always did this whenever he saw something really, really special. He had noticed how different things looked, depending on which eye was doing the looking. This way, he could take in an extraordinary sight from a multitude of different perspectives, almost all at once. He kept this unusual little habit from his brothers and sisters, so as to avoid earning himself the terrible name, "Blinky."

So, there Spider stood. Alone at the edge of a thin branch, and well out of the others' sight. He was blinking furiously at the gorgeous deepening orange colour, as the suns first rays slowly ripened. The lights above climbed up the far side of the bush, gradually piercing more, and more of the canopy above.

The gentle sway of the breeze was secretly choreographing the gaps in the leaves, creating an ever changing display overhead. The early morning mist caught the Sunbeams on their way down, creating mesmerising dancing shafts of light.

Spider tried to recall his mothers' rhyme, maybe then he would know what he should do next. All he could remember though was, "Long and Strong." He stretched out his leg and said, "Nooooo, strong, but not that long."

He looked at a branch. "Oooooh, that is very long, and super strong! But why, what, errrrrrrrr!"

He shook his fluffy head and said to himself, "That is absolutely no clue at all!"

Then, he remembered something else. "Fly and Sky!"

He knew what a fly was as he rubbed his tummy with three of his legs, but what was "SKY?"

This was not much help, so he thought long and hard again.

Then, one word popped into his head and, WHAM! The whole rhyme flashed back into his mind.

"HIGH"

"Build your web HIGH!"

Spiders eyes blinked across his face like flicked jelly, as he looked straight up. He stared at the carpet of lights above, that had fascinated him for as long as he could remember.

"They're high," he said to himself. Now, he knew exactly what he should do!

Chapter 3
The Big Picture

Spider did not look back once! He propelled himself upward, swiftly leaping from branch to branch. His excitement was almost boiling over, as the lights got closer and closer.

But when he finally broke through the final leaf, the dazzling brilliance of the clear spring sunlight totally blinded him. He staggered awkwardly backwards, completely losing his grip.

In that moment, some ancient instinct kicked in, and he lunged out with his abdomen. Even though he was unable to see anything, he managed to attach a strand of silk to a leaf as he fell past it.

Spider plunged back down into the depths of the bush, from whence he had come. Frantically reeling out his silken safety line as he dropped.

Rapidly he picked up speed as he plummeted further, he was only brave enough to keep one of his recovering blurred eyes open. Even with one impaired eye, he could see the seething mass of his siblings, as he zoomed directly at them.

Blinky clenched on the brakes, just in time!

Boing Boing Boing.

Spider eventually bounced to a stop, barely a centimetre above his still bickering swarm of brothers and sisters.

"Hello," he said. The Spiderlings all squealed in surprise at the unexpected voice from above, briskly scattering in all directions.

Blinky gently lowered himself down onto the branch with surprising skill, considering it was the first time he had done it. Eventually, after the panic had subsided, the others slowly gathered around him.

(They were all silent, for a change.)

Spider knew that they wanted to hear what had happened to him up there, but having all those eyes staring at him in curious anticipation, instantly stalled his words.

This made his mind go completely blank!

After a brief but very uncomfortable silence, all the Spiderlings spoke together, in perfect unison.

"WELL, GO ON THEN!"

They were completely taken aback, by how much noise they made when they all spoke at once.

That was most definitely the first time it had happened!

It was so loud that they all started to get worried, what if one of those scary predators their mother had spoken of heard them. Maybe something terrible was about to come crashing through the leaves, making an easy meal of them all in one big mouthful.

Spiders voice was still a little bit lost, so instead of speaking he just pointed up at the lights with two of his legs, and all of his eyes.

They all responded simultaneously again.

"WHAAAAAAT!"

But this time it was even louder than before, and quickly followed by a unanimous, "shhhhh shhhhh shhhh shhhh"

In the following silence, Spider finally found his courage. He described the blinding experience he had had in the branches high above, the Spiderlings all gasped in unison. Then silently prodded each other with one foot, while covering their mouths with another.

They started quietly murmuring to each other about Spiders story, but as they all tried to have their say, the volume quickly rose into that illegible hum once more.

Spider was a bit distracted by the Yellowish red circle, that had been burnt into the centre of all 8 of his eyes. Strangely, it stayed right in the middle, no matter which way he looked. Even though whatever it was up there had inflicted this odd symptom upon him, all he really wanted to do was go back up for another look.

So, as the others jostled to be heard, Spider slipped quietly back up his silk thread.

He gave it a couple of quick tugs, checking that it was still firmly attached to the leaf, way up at the top of the bush.

It was, so up he went.

As he climbed higher and higher he could still hear the others below, the debate was quickly escalating into a fully blown argument. Finally he reached his destination, but this time he carefully pushed the last leaf aside.

And then he saw it!

It took quite a few moments for his eyes to adjust to the bright light, as the most extraordinary sight slowly came into focus. A towering cityscape rose high up into the clouds, as the yellow sunlight shimmered off the windows of the numerous skyscrapers. It was an awe inspiring vision, which left his mouth gaping wide open in disbelief.

Spider suddenly felt extremely small, which of course he was.

As he sat bewitched by the mind blowing view, he started blinking at it, passionately, but slowly. He didn't want to miss anything from any angle, but he was far too engrossed in capturing the moment, to pay due care and attention to his more immediate surroundings.

Chapter 4
Blinky and Bill

While Spider was still obsessing over the view, a bellowing breeze suddenly roared up all around him. The powerful rush of wind was accompanied by a deep, rhythmical pounding.

Spider was struggling to keep his grip in the increasingly fierce gust when.

CRRRRRRASH!

An enormous bird landed on the branch right next to him, it was a great big Tit!

The huge Blue Tit stood leaning over him, bobbing its head from side to side. It was glaring straight at him with one eye, and then the other.

Spider was so terrified that he started blinking even faster than ever, and in an increasingly uncontrollable pattern.

The bird wobbled its head once more, taking in this bizarre sight with its other eye again, before bursting into laughter.

"Alright there Blinky?" It squawked in between giggles. Its wings wrapped around its belly, in a futile attempt to contain its laughter.

Drat, thought Spider. The very name I've been so desperately trying to avoid being given. But I suppose it's better to have a name I don't like, than to be a birds' breakfast.

"Are, are, are you going to eat me?" Spider stammered nervously.

"Not now!" chuckled the bird, "how could I eat something that has made me laugh so much? You've made my day already, and the Sun is only just up."

"Besides, you are barely a snack. Not even close to half a beak full!"

The Tit introduced himself. "I'm Billingsworth Blue Tit, the 3rd." He announced holding his wing tip proudly to his chest, in a rather stately manner. "But everyone calls me Bill."

Bill offered Spider the underneath of his right wing.

"Give me some Plum son!"

"What's a Plum?" Replied Spider.

"Some plum," you know some plumage! Tickle my feathers, whack my wing. That's how Blue Tits say hello," he explained.

Spider tapped his two fluffy front feet on Bills outstretched wing.

"Hello Bill, I'm Warrior." Said Spider in his deepest voice, and puffing out his chest as much as he could.

"Whatever you say Blinky," Bill said, starting to snigger again.

Double drat, thought Spider.

After Bill had managed to calm himself enough to speak, he asked. "So Blinky, what are you doing up here anyway?"

"Well," I'm trying to find the highest place possible to build my web, so I can catch as many flies as I can!"

Bill looked all around for a moment, then he poked a wing out towards the highest tower within sight, before saying. "Well, that's the tallest thing around here for miles."

Blinkys' eyes flickered wildly as he scanned the towering skyscraper from top to bottom, before confidently stating.

"Then that's where I'm headed!"

"You sure about that Blinky?" Bill squawked. "It's a very long way up!"

"YES!" Said Blinky resolutely.

"Well, you certainly sound like you've made your mind up. Hop up on my back, I'll give you a lift up to the highest terrace. That should at least give you a good start!"

Bill swung his wing out in a graceful bowing motion. "Jump up then, but hold on tight, I go fast!"

Blinky climbed carefully onto Bills back, gripping on tightly with all of his legs.

"Ready?" Said Bill

"Aaaaaaand, we're off!"

With that Bill Tipped his right wing over, dropping sharply off the branch, he was heading straight down!

Blinky squealed with terror, as the ground came rushing towards him. Then just a few meters above the grass, Bill twisted his shoulders back and they swooped upwards. They were now racing towards the Eastern edge of the parks boundary walls.

With a few gentle beats of his wings, Bill gained just enough height to clear the wall. They soared effortlessly up, breezing over the busy road that circled the small city park.

Blinkys' blink couldn't keep up with all the amazing things that rushed by, they were just going too fast.

As they approached the building, Bill caught an up draft of hot air as it rose up the side of the skyscraper. He rode it all the way up to the terrace, without even needing to flap his wings once.

Blinky so desperately wanted to have a good long blink, at all the sights whizzing by below.

But he was enjoying the thrill of the ride so much, he soon stopped caring.

Bill made a very gentle landing on the outside terrace of a luxury restaurant, they were now already at least a third of the way up the skyscraper.

"Here you go Blinky, I'm afraid this is as high as I can drop you off. It's the Blue Tits ball tonight, and I'm already VERY late!"

"Good luck and be careful!"

"Ooooh before I go," Bill continued.

"Here's some advice for you. DO NOT go up to the roof! There are lots of birds living up there, they will surely eat you up without a second thought!"

"There is one thing you could say to a bird though, if you do get cornered and have the chance to speak."

Bill sang out something in Beakish, and after repeating the melody a few times he said.

"Memorise this Blinky! It's a special phrase that means you are a friend of the birds. If they hear it, they shouldn't harm you."

Blinky tried to replicate the series of whistles and wheeps to the best of his ability. But to his ears, it didn't sound even slightly similar.

"Good enough," Bill squawked. "Just keep repeating it over and over, you never know, it may just save your life one day!"

"I've got to be going now," said Bill. As they stood on a beautiful oak and iron table with a panoramic view. "Once again good luck, I hope we will meet again one day. I'll see if I can find you up there next time I'm passing."

Bill held out his wing for Blinky to give him some more, "plum." And with a series of quick flaps, he was off into the blue spring sky.

Blinky was now all alone. He stood staring straight up, the seemingly infinite wall of glass stretched up further than his eyes could see.

Once again he felt very, VERY small!

He decided not to think about how hard this journey would be, it was what he had to do!

So best to just go for it!

Chapter 5
Maternal Instincts

The first part of the climb was actually fairly straight forward, or straight up in this particular case. He could easily climb up the metal strips that surrounded each window pane, and he was actually making fairly swift progress.

But as he got higher, sudden gusts of wind started to come unannounced, and they pulled at him with grip levering force.

The temperature dropped with each minute that passed, Blinky had never felt such a biting cold before. He even started to shiver, which is not a good thing when you're climbing!

It was just after midday when Blinky stopped for a rest, taking the chance to look out at the increasingly magnificent view.

Just as he turned to continue his epic climb, the Sun started to pass over the top of the building. Suddenly unleashing its full force directly down onto him. Again, by accident, he looked straight into it. And again, he was completely blinded and had to close all of his eyes shut tight.

After a few moments, he eventually regained enough of his sight to carry on climbing. So, squinting into the light, he continued onwards and upwards. Blinky was now pulling an entirely new funny face as he tried to look around, above, or under the red circle burnt into the middle of his eyes.

With his vision impaired, Blinky didn't notice the thick web above him. It spanned the entire corner of the window he was climbing up. It wasn't until his foot touched the web, that he realised the danger he was in. But of course, by then, it was already too late!

In the blink of an eye, a HUGE garden spider shot out of the corner of the window. It accelerated with each bound as it raced straight down towards him.

"WAIT, WAIT, I'm not a fly," Blinky pleaded in a desperate attempt to slow the spiders instinctive pounce, But the well-rehearsed attack was already underway!

As the predator rapidly approached, Blinkys last hope was to bail! He quickly fastened a silk anchor to the window with his bum, and launched himself backwards as he had when he had fallen from the shrub earlier.

His fate now rested completely, on the strength of the bond between his silk and the glass.

After free falling for a couple of metres, Blinky tentatively and progressively clenched himself to a stop. Grateful that his sticky lifeline had saved him once again.

He swung back into the window pane where he had rested earlier, taking a few long deep breaths and thinking he was clear of danger.

HE WASN'T!

With one abrupt, powerful yank. He was pulled clean off the glass, and dragged back up the window bottom first. The beast above had untethered his life line, it began reeling him swiftly back up towards it's waiting fangs.

Blinky wriggled his legs in panic, trying to release more silk to lower himself further from the garden spiders gaping jaws. But his silk reserves were almost depleted, and the hungry spider above was using 6 of its legs to wind his silk in. Even if he did have more silk, he was going up much faster than he could spin it out.

As Blinky got closer and closer to being lunch, he swung himself upwards to have one last blink at his inevitable fate and said out loud.

"I'm sorry mother, I did my best, but I didn't make it"

Almost immediately, Blinky saw a complete transformation in the predators expression. It was in that split of a second, the garden spiders entire demeanour switched. Flashing from fierce and aggressive, to soft and tender. But more importantly, it was decelerating.

Blinky knew he had to think fast, he was definitely on the menu. He was also so small that he would have no chance, if the massive arachnid did choose to eat him.

He used this moment to quickly introduce himself. "I'm Blinky," he said, demonstrating his infamous blink.

"That's how I got my name," he followed. Giving another awkward eye wobble, just to prove his point. He was hoping, that maybe like Bill this spider also had a sense of humour.

The gigantic, fully grown garden spider looked rather confused for a moment. But at least it had not eaten him, yet.

Eventually she responded "I'm Arraneous."

"You should be more careful where you are treading young Spiderling, I very nearly wrapped you up for my tea!"

After nearly collapsing with relief, Blinky finally said.

"Thanks for not!"

"What's with those eyes by the way?" asked Arraneous, "Bit weird that is!"

"That's my way of capturing an extraordinary sight in as many ways as possible before it passes me by," explained Blinky. "There have already been so many amazing sights so far in my life, I've been blinking a lot."

Blinky hoped that what he had said made sense. It was hard to be sure, as Arraneous now had an even more puzzled glaze in her eyes.

"Hmmmmmmmmmm," hummed Arraneous slowly. "That certainly is an interesting way of looking at things! I'm always too busy worrying about where my next meal is coming from, to even think about enjoying what's around me in the moment."

"But now you mention it, it is a pretty amazing view from up here. I've just got too used to it to notice anymore!"

She tried to replicate Blinkys blink a couple of times while looking out over the city, but she couldn't quite manage it. She just kept closing all of her eyes at the same time, her mouth scrunched up as it wiggled from one side of her face to the other. It was at least in perfect sync with her blink, as she tried to keep some eyes open and some closed.

Blinky chuckled and said, "I can kind of see why people find it so amusing when they look at me doing that now!"

"I really should be going," said Blinky as he looked back up to the distant summit above. "I still have a very long way to go."

"Thank you again for not eating me!"

Arraneous looked down at him and smiled as she said. "I left my children many months ago, because I was told that was what I was supposed to do. I have no idea where they are, or what has happened to them. It made me sad for a while, not knowing what had become of them. Sometimes when I'm waiting in my web for a fly to come along, I day dream of my children. I like to imagine them having big webs in a safe place, where the flies gather in swarms. Maybe imagining that is better than knowing the truth."

"I just climbed up here and settled back into life as a lone hunter again, I would like to think that some of them are like you, having adventures and finding their own way in the world."

"There are many dangers up here, especially at night. Stay in the cracks as much as you can Blinky. The Bats come at dusk and they will snatch you away without warning, if they can find you!"

"And be careful of other spiders too, although I doubt you will see any that have climbed higher than we are now."

Blinky gave a final wave goodbye, before turning back towards the piercing rays of the sun. It was now in full view, without even a wisp of cloud to offer some shelter from its scorching glare.

Chapter 6
A Perilous Climb

After a few hours had passed, apart from the occasional short rest, Blinky kept on climbing higher and higher. He was sure he was at least halfway now, and felt a boost of confidence from the thought. The Suns power was finally starting to lose its edge, it had already completed two thirds of its journey across the sky as it arced over toward the West.

This was all so new to Blinky, he really had no clue what all these things around him were. The only thing he was sure of now, was that the burning ball in the sky was the cause of the lights he had been so fascinated by. It was certainly an incredible spectacle, way beyond his wildest of guesses when he was back in the bush.

The repetitive movement of climbing and then climbing some more, left a lot of time for Blinkys' mind to wander. He started thinking about how his siblings were getting on, he wondered if they were all still in the bush squabbling. Or had they settled on a plan at last?

He was so distracted by his thoughts, that he hadn't noticed the sun was about to set behind him. It was only when he caught a glimpse of the deepening orange disc in the reflection of a window, that be turned to face it and gasped.

This was easily the most beautiful thing he had seen on his quest so far!

The distant clouds were wrapped in a tangerine blanket, and he could see through a small gap in the buildings, what looked like huge trees. There was one especially tall tree stealing the last of the Suns reddening rays, it proudly stood high and wide above all the others.

As the Sun closed the curtains on its daily performance in the most spectacular way, Blinky took a few moments to give his first sunset the Blink it deserved.

He was far too busy blinking away at the ever changing display of light, to notice there were a pair of Bats darting around erratically below him.

They were using their amazing in built sonar to scan the skies for dinner. But the first Blinky knew of them was when one whooshed right past him, it was no more than 2 cm from the end of his nose.

He was so alarmed that he let out a short YELP in surprise, this unfortunately confirmed to the bat that there was indeed something to eat there.

In response, it quickly banked sharply around for another pass.

Blinky managed to squeeze himself tight into the window sill as far as he could, he was just in time, the Bats claws frantically scratched at the glass as it passed. Blinky tucked his legs tightly into the window sill, he was safe, for now. There he stayed motionless all night, completely frozen with fear.

Blinky was woken up early by the distant morning call of the birds below. A faint glow slowly crept over the city, as the tide of light turned once again. The darkness was gradually vanquished, and forced to shelter in the shadows, during the rule of the day.

It was a particularly beautiful sunrise, unfortunately Blinky was on the wrong side of the building to witness its full glory. Besides he was still so worried about the Bats, he only dared to poke one eye out from behind cover.

When the dawn had dismissed enough of the night for Blinky to see clearly a good distance. He tentatively ventured out further, scanning all around with each step he took.

There was no sign of the black winged monsters, so he began to climb again. Keeping his wits about him this time, just in case some other deadly fiend was forthcoming.

Chapter 7
You CAN do it!

By the time the Sun was about to pass over the top of the building again, Blinky could finally see the top at last. He was so, so close!

But wait, he thought. What was it Bill had said about going to the top?

"Go to the top? Don't go to the top?" Blinky questioned himself out loud once, and then a couple more times in his head.

Welllllll...... He pondered to himself. There's been so much danger out here, how could it possibly be any worse up there?

"Besides," he finally concluded out loud. "I've come all this way, surely there's no harm in having a little peek."

So, with one last big heave, Blinky hoisted himself up and over the ledge, instantly proving himself wrong! There most definitely could be harm in having a "little," peek!

There before him, spread out over the entire skyscrapers rooftop, was a whole flock of Pigeons. They were absolutely everywhere!

Three of them spotted him straight away, immediately taking to flight. They were coming straight at him!

Blinky, struck by a sudden panic, desperately tried to remember the Beakish phrase Bill had taught him. But time was running out, and running out fast!

Using the leap and line trick again would be of no use this time. The birds were to many and too fast, they would catch him easily.

Blinky frantically scanned around, desperately searching for somewhere, anywhere to hide. He spotted an empty aluminium can, it was sitting upright on the floor just in front of him. It was close, but it was still a massive leap for a tiny spider like him.

As the Pigeons rapidly closed in, a snap decision was needed.

"That will have to Doooooooooooooooo!"

Blinky jumped, wailing as if it were a battle cry. Bravely he leapt off the ledge with all his might, rocketing towards the tiny distant black bullseye. He stretched all of his legs out in front of him as far as he could. Just in case that little bit of extra reach, made the definitive difference between life or death.

To Blinky in this moment time seemed to pass so slowly, that he felt like a helpless spectator to the action unravelling all around him.

The first Pigeon soon arrived, swooping past just above his head. It was unable to alter its trajectory quickly enough to intercept the flying spider. But the second one had much more time to adjust its course. Its' beak snapped loudly shut, just millimetres above Blinkys head.

The can made a loud KLANG!

Bullseye!

Blinky shot straight through the hole in the top, bouncing twice off the sides before landing with a squelchy splat at the bottom. The can still had some juice in it slowly drying out at the bottom, it was really, really sticky.

Blinky had to use all of his legs to peel himself away from the thick sweet orange residue.

After he managed to free himself, just outside the can a heated conversation was going on in Beakish. He didn't understand what the muffled voices were saying, but he was pretty sure it was all about him.

But how could he possibly get all the way back up to the top, he really wanted to see exactly what was going on?

He tested his grip on the inside walls of the can, to see if he had any grip on it at all. The sweet orange stuff that was now stuck all over his feet, had an unexpected side effect. Not only was it very very tasty, but it also made his feet sticky enough to climb up the slippery metal cylinder.

So, with each step making a sound a like pulling cello tape off a carpet, Blinky steadily unpeeled and re-stuck his way up the can.

All the time he was desperately racking his brains, trying to remember the phrase in Beakish Bill had taught him.

He felt like his life depended on it, and it did!

When he finally reached the hole of light at the top of the can, he gingerly squeezed a couple of eyes over the edge for a peek. Two very animated Pigeons came into view. Distracted by the two jostling birds, as they shouted and flapped at each other. Blinky didn't notice the other, not so frisky Pigeon staring straight at him.

After a side mouthed "Pssssst," and a forceful prod of its' wing, so were the other two.

All three started silently hopping towards him, they each wore a friendly smile as they approached, but their eyes told a very different story. Even with his extremely limited life experience, Blinky instinctively knew that he was in big trouble.

Now was his chance. As they got closer, Blinky took a deep breath, grabbed onto the ring pull, and went for it.

At the top of his voice he belted out the sentence in Beakish, or at least what he could remember of it.

"Burrrrr burrrrr tweet whistle clack clack tweet!"

The Pigeons all cocked their heads sideways, as if they were dodging bullets. But still they carried on moving forwards.

Blinky tried again, but this time with an even deeper breath. He gave it all of the force that he could muster and let rip.

"BURRRRR, BURRRRR, TWEET WHISTLE CLACK CLACK, TWEET!"

This time the response was instantaneous, the Pigeons burst out into laughter. They were all laughing so hard that they began falling about, having to grab onto each other for support. I think it's fair to say, the Pigeons were in hysterics.

Blinky popped his whole head out of the can, so he could have a proper look at what would later become, a familiar sight. As he watched, completely bewildered by the show that was going on. One of the Pigeons, gasping for breath, clumsily tripped over backwards. The still laughing Pigeon landed hard with a thud on his back, this only made the other two laugh even more.

The Pigeon which was now lying on his back was the first to pull himself together, he swivelled his head round his shoulders into a very bizarre and uncomfortable looking angle. Eventually ending up staring straight at Blinky out of the corner of one of his eyes.

Eventually he said, "Didn't mean to laugh at you little fella, but do you have any idea what you just said?" He was clearly struggling not to start giggling again.

"Well," started Blinky. I'm not completely sure, but it was meant to be something like. I'm a friend of Birds, please don't eat me!"

"Nah mate," said the Pigeon. "What you actually said was, I mean the exact translation of it is this."

The big Pigeon stood himself up straight. He flicked his wing across the front of his face, revealing a completely straight face after it had passed.

Then taking a deep breath, he started.

"You said. I can't possibly accept this strawberry flavoured Wibble, because my feet smell like a dogs old toy. And by the way, I'm late for lunch with the king of the waffles."

Blinky actually lifted his foot to his nose to check, and he asked. "What is a old dogs toy? And what does it smell like?"

The Pigeons were still on the brink of hysteria, and this was too much for them to take. The other two fell over in a heap on the floor, laughing so hard they could barely breathe Thud "Pahhhaaahahahaaa" Thud, "giggle giggle giggle."

The one who had just got up fell back over again, he just rolled back and forth holding his tummy saying. "Stop stop, it's too much! Hahahahhahaaaaa"

"You don't Hooohoo hoooo, know what a wi wi wibble is either do you? Pahhahahahahahaaaa."

Nor should you either young Spiderling. And before you ask, no I'm not telling you. "Hoooooh hahahaaaaaahahahahaaaaaaa."

"Who on earth told you to say that anyway?" Asked the closest Pigeon. "I'd like to shake his wing for a brilliant gag like that," The other two nodded in agreement, still on the floor chuckling.

"It was a Blue Tit called Billingsworth," Blinky announced. "I met him yesterday on my way here, and he helped me a lot. Apparently I'm far too small and way too funny to eat. He tried to teach me that phrase in Beakish before we parted. He said that it could save my life if I was ever attacked by birds!"

"It did!" Interrupted the nearest Pigeon, with a wink.

"When you say too funny to eat," added the Pigeon. "You certainly tickled us, but what exactly did you do to make old Bill laugh enough to help you, instead of eat you?"

"I blinked at him," answered Blinky quietly. That's why he gave me the name Blinky"

All three Pigeons immediately sprung onto their bellys, making a grey semicircle of eyes and feathers around the can. They sat attentively with their chins resting on their wings and looking expectantly at the small spider perched on top of the can.

"Go on then!" They chanted......

"Dooooooo it, pleeeeeease... Just once..... For us!"

Eventually Blinky agreed. He looked down at his eager Pigeon audience, and demonstrated his unusual memory making technique.

The Pigeons were quiet for a split second, completely taken aback by the bonkers display they had just witnessed. Then after looking at each other for a few silent glances, they all burst into uncontrollable laughter again.

As the Pigeons rolled about screaming with laughter, all Blinky could do was jump silently down from the can top stage, and walk off. He thought it best to go and look for a quiet little corner to hide in, at least until the Pigeons had calmed down enough to make some sense.

Once Blinky had settled into a safe dark little spot, he quickly got used to the background noise from the boisterous Pigeons, and realised just how tired he was.

So, well before it was even starting to get dark, the tired little Spider drifted off into a long deep sleep.

Chapter 8
It's a Pigeons Life

It was still dark when Blinky finally woke up. Little did he realise that while he was fast asleep, word had spread of his name, and the reason why he had it. During his slumber, the entire flock had spent hours attempting to imitate how they imagined his Blink to look. But it could never have the same amusing effect, when performed by only two eyes.

So, even though he didn't know anybody on the rooftop yet, he was already kind of a celebrity.

After emerging Blinky quickly drew a crowd of expectant fans, they were all clearly hoping for a performance. "Good morning Blinky" Said a friendly big brown bird.

"I'm Carl," he continued with slight bow. "And on behalf of the whole rooftop crew, I would like to welcome you as an honorary member of the flock."

"Errr thanks," replied Blinky. He was still a little sleepy, and rather puzzled by all the unexpected attention.

"We were all wondering... If you wouldn't mind of course that is, showing us your blink? We've all been trying it out, and I think Pauly is the only one who has nearly got it. Show him Pauly!"

A young skinny Pigeon stepped forward and blinked his best. But as Pigeons have eyes on either side of their heads, he had to twist himself from side to side as he did it. Which in truth, made him look more than a little bit bonkers.

"Ok, said Blinky." Firstly he explained why he blinked in such an unusual way, to which they all went "Ahhhhh." Then he casually hopped up onto the top of the can, so they could all see the performance clearly. The Pigeons quickly gathered round eagerly, and waited in anticipation for the show to begin.

Blinky gave it his all, wobbling his eyes in an elaborate pattern. He blinked in a sequence that started at the top left eye, then right.

Working alternate sides down to the bottom, then back up again. He rocked his blink from all left to all right. Finally he finished on a full circle finale, one way and then the other. The Pigeons went absolutely wild, whooping and clapping. "That's BRILLIANT," they all cheered loudly, unable to help giggling a bit too.

As the satisfied crowd slowly started to disperse, the three Pigeons from earlier wiggled their way through to the front.

"Morning Blinks." Said one of them, "Well, I suppose introductions are in order. I'm Dave, this is Steve, and the big quiet speckled one at the back is Franky."

"Franky doesn't say much." Dave continued. "But when he does say something, it's usually something that's worth hearing."

"Are you hungry? You must be starving after climbing all that way."

As if to answer Daves question, Blinkys stomach rumbled angrily.

"I'm famished, I can't remember the last time I had something to eat. It'll take me a while to make a web though, are there many flies up here? We are so high up now, surely there must be swarms of them?"

Blinky looked around the rooftop, he was expecting to see at least a few flies buzzing around.

"Well, while you were asleep we had a little chat. Franky and I think we've found the perfect place for you! I'll show you later".

Steve who always has trouble keeping quiet for long, jumped into the conversation. "You woke up at just the right time, the night shift will be back soon. They always bring lots of tasty treats! Trust me, you're going to love human food! And the Sun will be properly up soon, if we go over to the eastern edge you can see it rise in all it's glory."

As they headed over to the East side of the building, Dave explained how the flock had taken to living up here, many years ago. "It was the idea of a very wise and insightful Pigeon called Woody. He suggested that if we all worked together, we would be safer and happier."

"Woody couldn't bear to see how some Pigeons struggled to survive on the streets alone. With age or injury making it hard to get to the food, before it was all gone. It can be a tough and lonely life down there."

"This way the ones who aren't able to easily look for food, can stay up here in safety. There are many, many useful things to do around the rooftop. Like sorting and storing the food, and preparing entertainment for the foragers when they return from their shift."

Steve jumped in again "There really is more than enough for everyone down on the streets, the humans throw so much good food away. There is often so much to choose from, sometimes we even come back up with a menu and ask what everyone wants."

"That's amazing," said Blinky thoughtfully. "Why doesn't everyone live like that?"

"Woody said, that long ago when he used to live in the forest, he met a wise old owl that told him lots of interesting stories. He told him that some animals work together like that as a team, for the benefit of all. It works pretty well for us, we always have everything that we need."

"Nothing ever bothers us up here, except this one human in a bright Orange jacket. He comes sometimes and plays around in the big silver boxes over there, but he doesn't take much notice of us."

"That was his drink can you jumped in earlier. What was it, Orange flavour?" Blinky had no idea what an Orange was, so he just nodded in agreement. "Good stuff that is!"

Dave stepped forward, which Steve knew meant for him to be quiet. "Anyway enjoy the sunrise, I'll go and check out the evenings haul as it comes in. If you're lucky there will be some cookies, I'll grab you one as long as Franky doesn't get there first."

"Mmmmm Cookies." Franky mumbled to himself.

Blinky sat on the eastern ledge, with Steve and Franky by his side. They quietly watched as the horizon slowly lightened, signalling the imminent arrival of the burning disc in the sky.

Steve and Franky weren't watching the sunrise, they saw it every single day. Besides, watching Blinky taking in the view in his very special way, was far more entertaining.

Chapter 9
Cookies Rule OK

The Suns' rays quickly spread out over the whole city, and the night shift of Pigeons was returning to the rooftop. There was some sort of a commotion building up over in the middle of the roof, the three of them all turned to see what was going on.

Then, Blinky saw Dave flapping up from the middle of the bustling mass of grey feathers. There was a long red shiny cylinder in his beak. He was also being followed closely by two other Pigeons, they didn't seem at all happy.

Dave dipped sharply over the ledge, and he was out of sight before the others could get a feather on him.

A few minutes later after the search for Dave had been called off, they heard a quiet. "Hooohoo."

It was coming from a dark corner behind them.

Then, out of the shadows appeared Dave, with a nearly full packet of double choc chip cookies in his beak.

The usually slow Franky, suddenly moved so fast he nearly left his feathers behind. Dave had to throw a cookie at his head, just to stop him from crashing into him.

"Shhhhhh Franky," hissed Dave. "If the others see us then we're done for."

He needn't have said anything though. Franky was busy rubbing his head with one wing, while slowly pushing the cookie that had hit him into his mouth with the other. He wasn't going to cause any trouble, well for at least five minutes anyway. Dave then said with authority, "Blinky's only small, two cookies will be more than enough for him, we can split the rest!" Dave was clearly the leader of the trio.

The three Pigeons slipped into the shadowy corner with their favourite dinner, they had devoured the rest of the packet before Blinky even got halfway through a quarter of his first one. "This is absolutely delicious," he said, blinking slowly at the cookie in delight.

As the sweet chocolate started melting in his mouth, he couldn't even blink anymore. For once he just closed his eyes, and enjoyed the exquisite flavour as it flooded his taste buds.

Of course this wasn't news to the Pigeons, they were already eyeballing the cookie Blinky was nibbling. Clearly he was eating way too slowly for them, but Blinky was blissfully ignorant as he savoured every sumptuous bite.

When Blinky finished his mouthful and opened his eyes, he noticed all the Pigeons were watching him eat. "Even though these are gorgeous," Blinky started. "I just can't fit any more in, here, you three share what's left, that's half each.

I really would still like to catch some flies though, after all that is the reason I climbed all the way up here!"

"Oh yes, that's right." Mumbled Steve, with half a cookie in his mouth. Franky found just the place for you to build your web, hop this way"

Still chewing, Steve bounced along the wall of the skyscraper. He headed over to the Western edge, and jumped up onto the ledge. "Look over here Blinky," he said bobbing his head over the precipice.

When Blinky finally caught up and hauled himself onto the ledge, he peered cautiously over, and saw a big metal box hanging from the side of the building. There was an old air conditioning vent bolted to the outside of the wall, it jutted precariously over the dizzying drop to the streets below. Clearly, it was in a state of disrepair. And judging by the rust that covered it, it hadn't been used for quite a while.

Dave started to explain what it was, but Blinky was far to distracted by the unbelievable view.

There, stretched out before him, was the wildest array of buildings, old and new. With a wide river snaking through the city, slithering off as far as the eye could see in both directions.

Blinky turned and asked, "what's that over there Steve? There's a huge green gap in the buildings, it looks like lots of really big trees."

Steve followed Blinkys' gaze, "Yes it is, there's a huge park down there. Looks close doesn't it, and by wing it's only a few minutes flap away. But it is actually quite some distance for you wingless types.

It's a really nice place, there are cool fountains to bath in when it's hot, and always lots of nice people chucking bread about. If only they knew, it was cookies we really wanted!"

After a few minutes of Blinkys eyes going bananas at the view, Dave used his wing to send a wake up wave of air in his direction. "You'll have plenty of time to take in the scenery, here have a look at this. It's perfect, well done for finding it Franky!"

Dave stretched out his left leg and tapped his foot on the top of the big metal box, it rang out like a bell as he struck it.

BONGGGGGG BONGGGGGGGGGGGGGGG.

After the vibrating box finally fell silent, Franky had something to say. "The human that comes up here, he hasn't touched this one for years. He only ever goes near the big shiny ones over there, so he shouldn't bother you in here."

Dave stepped right out onto the old metal box, he jumped up and down a few times to test its strength. BONNNGGG BONGGG BONGGGGGGGGG, replied the metal.

"Careful shouted Blinky, you might fall"

"I can fly!" Said Dave chuckling. "Falling isn't quite the drama for me as it would be for you. See it's strong!" Dave stooped down out over the edge of the box, all that remained visible of him was his upturned tail feather. He tapped his beak on the metal grill that covered a big rusty fan. Ting, Ting, Ting responded the antique steel.

"Nice and safe in there," added Franky with a nod.

"Shielded from the wind, and wandering beaks." Stated Dave. In fact the only thing that could get to you in there, would be another Spider!"

Blinky looked up and asked, "Are there any?"

Dave hopped back off the box, fluttering down from the ledge onto the smooth grey rooftop. He gestured with his wing for Blinky to follow.

"Better to chat down here out of the wind, it feels like it's picking up a bit. At this height the wind can come on sudden and strong. So always make sure you have a good grip on something whenever you're near the edge!"

Blinky launched himself down onto the rooftop, and nestled in behind a thick metal pipe. The others all lined up against the wall and huddled in tight, away from the winds sight.

Dave was right. Almost immediately the wind picked up, it quickly went from a whistle to a howl, whipping its way around the skyscraper. It was as if it were late, and annoyed that the building was blocking its path.

Once everyone was settled, Dave answered Blinkys question.

"There has only been one that I know of who has made it up this far, his name was BONGO.

He really became part of the crew, one of the family. He was up here with us until his very last day."

"Bongo popped out of a vent one morning, with absolutely no idea where he was. The only thing he did know, was that he was absolutely terrified of heights. Bit of an unfortunate place to end up really, he never ever once went anywhere near the edge."

Steve had been waiting to get involved, he shuffled around and made his move on the conversation. "Oooh let me tell him the story, please!"

"Go on then," said Dave rolling his eyes.

Franky just looked at Steve and said.

"Do it!"

Chapter 10
The story of Bongo

Narrated by Stephen Gurnbeak (Steve the Pigeons full name)

"A long time ago. In a land, far far away. There lived a house Spider, called Bongo."

"Bongo was quite happy, he lived in the bedroom of a cosy country cottage. He would spend all night running around the floor, looking for things to eat."

"But one day. His afternoon nap was rudely interrupted, by lots of loud banging and the shuffling around of heavy things. All the noise forced him out of his hiding place, and he ended up accidentally falling into a big open cardboard box."

"Unfortunately he then got cello taped in. The next time he saw the light of day, he was on the 98th floor of this skyscraper. It was only two floors below the penthouse apartment, with floor to ceiling windows. The view from there is so good, it could keep you blinking for at least a week."

"Sadly for poor old Bongo, that's when he realised just how scared of heights he was."

"The apartment was all so new and shiny, there were absolutely no places for him to hide. He then took one look at the view out of the window, and shot straight up the nearest air vent."

"Eventually, he popped out of that vent over there. He landed right on top of Kevs' head, who was just about to take a big bite out of a sandwich." All the Pigeons had a little giggle about the funny memory.

"Naturally, Kev completely freaked out. He did look pretty funny though, jumping around wearing Bongo like a wig."

Dave spluttered, unable to keep his laugh in. "Bongo Wig, Hahahahahaaa, nice one Steve."

Steve smiled, waited a moment for silence, then continued.

"Just like you Blinky, he nearly got eaten up straight away. And the second Kev managed to get him off his head, Bongo leapt straight back into the vent and hid. All Kev's shouting and dancing around, quickly drew a crowd of curious Pigeons to the scene."

"Most of them just thought Kev had made up another new dance move. They felt that he deserved to be politely informed, that the world might not be ready for moves like that, not just yet."

"While we were explaining to the others what had really happened, Bongo was still sitting in the dark vent, scared stiff."

"Of course, poor Bongo couldn't understand a tweet of Beakish. So naturally he assumed the conversation going on outside, was some kind of plot for his demise."

"The only thing Bongo could think of to do, was to start banging out a rhythm on the floor and walls of the vent he was hiding in. Luckily, he had picked up some wicked grooves, just by listening to music played in the house he used to live in. By using his many legs as drumsticks, he could actually put some pretty complex beats together."

"Turns out he was not only a house spider by name, but also by nature. With a library of beats that catchy, he quickly found a place up here with us. We even gathered up a few old cans for him, along with anything else we found on the streets that made an interesting noise when banged."

"Bongo, was absolutely brilliant at playing the cans! Us Pigeons are all feathers and beaks, so there's no way we can play any instruments at all. Apart from the Pecksechord that is. Although Boris was rather skilled on that, it was always Bongos' Bongo's, that got the tailfeathers twerking!"

All the Pigeons nodded, giving each other a sad glance at the thought of their old friend.

It was Dave that finally broke the sad silence, by saying. "Right, lets get going lads, we're on the day shift today. We had better go and find something good to bring back, seen as we pinched all the cookies earlier."

"Blinky, it's probably best you stay here and make yourself comfortable in your new home. There will still be quite a few Pigeons just coming back, they may not know that you're one of us now. There is always a chance they might gobble you up without asking, especially if you smell like cookies!"

So off the three birds flapped, already scanning the streets below in search of potential hot spots. They shouted out what they saw to each other, as they circled down to the city streets on the hunt for food.

Chapter 11
Room with a View

Blinky had spent most of the day inside his air conditioning box, weaving himself a deluxe web hammock in between the fan and the wall. He had just finished it, when there was a loud BONG BONG BONG from above! Franky's big head arched down into view.

He had half a biscuit grasped in his beak, which he carefully lined up with a gap in the grill of the box. Then, before Blinky could get the word NO passed his lips, Franky flicked the cookie through with his beak.

The sweet semicircle bounced awkwardly on its edge, rolling right through the string of web that was holding up Blinkys new hammock. Now unattached, the silky seat immediately dropped down on one side. Blinky was left hanging upside down, dangling by two of his legs, with a very unimpressed look on his face.

"Thanks for that," Blinky said sarcastically.

"You're welcome," said Franky, in his usual slow manner. He was clearly completely oblivious of the damage he'd just done, and how much time and thought had gone into making it. "Cookies were Bongo's absolute favourite too," Franky added.

It wasn't the depth or speed of Franky's voice that made it odd. Although, he did talk quite slowly, and a lot deeper than the other Pigeons. It was more that his expression didn't change one bit when he was talking. It made no difference what he was talking about, he never seemed to show any emotion.

In fact, the whole experience of having a conversation with Franky, was strangely hypnotic. You couldn't help but to give him your absolute attention.

Franky sat up on top of the box, and just before popping another cookie in his beak, he said.

"I've been thinking...... Aaaaaaaannnnnnd"

Blinky had the feeling this was going to be a long one, so he got himself untangled, and the right way up.

"You could attach your webs, from the edge of the box to the buildings wall. Doing that all the way around, will maximise the available catchment surface!"

"Best way I can think of to catch the most flies. Happy hunting!"

At that Franky launched himself off the box. Diving first and then looping back up in a spiral, until he was coming straight back at Blinky. It was an impressive aerial display, and must have been quite thrilling. But Franky still had the same blank expression on his face, as he buzzed past so close to the top of the box his feathers dusted it.

Unfortunately for Blinky, the rush of air that followed, ripped off the last supporting silk strands. With nothing else holding up what was left of his hammock, the whole thing, including Blinky come crashing to the floor.

While Blinky carefully repaired his bed, he pondered over Frankys idea and thought to himself. He really is worth listening to, I can't think of a more effective solution.

So there was Blinky, finally settled into his new home way up in the sky! He could see the sunset every evening from his lofty balcony box, and he could not wait to Blink at the first one.

Chapter 12
Prisoner in Paradise

As the weeks passed by, Blinky got to know the whole flock pretty well. He still sat every evening, and watched the always unique sunset. But he didn't blink at it very often, not anymore.

In fact, now the only time he did blink in his special way, was to explain his name to newcomers, as they arrived at the tower top refuge.

He didn't even make webs to catch flies these days, despite the resounding success of Frankys' wall of web idea. Besides, the scrumptious food the Pigeons brought up every day was far, far tastier than any fly. So keeping the web maintained seemed like a waste of time, and silk. It soon fell to ruin, blown high and away to some distant land.

He did however, turn the inside of his box, into a wondrous Palace of silk. It had two strong and perfectly symmetrical winding tunnels, that lead up to a huge sphere of silk, suspended gracefully in the corner.

One night, after Blinky had eaten a bit too much cookie to sleep. He started to think about what other things he could use his silk for, besides building that is.

He remembered how he used to make pictures in webs when he was a Spiderling, so he tried to recreate in web some of the wonderful things he'd seen so far. It didn't take him long to perfect the skyline view outside his home, the panorama ran all the way along one side of the box.

Because of the 8 different angles Blinky always viewed things from, his silk creations came out with an incredible depth, so much so that they had an amazing 3d effect.

Eventually the inside of his home was filled with spectacular web landscapes, capturing some of the views he had blinked at. He even managed to spin pretty accurate portraits, showing some of the characters he had met along the way. Nobody else on the roof had the slightest clue that such an amazing gallery of silk, lay hidden inside the rusty old box.

Whenever Steve, Dave and Franky had the night off. They would all sit with their backs up against the wall, and regail Blinky with some of their stories from the streets.

On one particularly clear and warm night, Blinky and his three Pigeon friends were sitting together quietly, just gazing up at the stars. But Blinky had something on his mind that had been bothering him for a while now, so he had to get it off his chest.

"Did Bongo ever want to leave?" Blinky asked, turning to Steve.

Steve cocked his eye down, "you thinking of leaving Blinky?"

"Aren't you happy up here?"

Blinky took a few steps out from the wall, he turned to face his Pigeon friends and said.

"Yes, of course I'm happy. I love it here, and you guys are the best."

"It's just, when I look down there, at the big park in the distance." Blinky pointed over the wall to the far away expanse of green.

"Do you see that one really tall tree? Sometimes I look at it and I can't seem to help the feeling, that my journey is not meant to end here. Not just yet."

"Yes," said Dave eventually. "Bongo wanted more than anything to leave, he talked a lot about going back down to the ground. He wanted to seek out his own kind, and share the knowledge he had gained up here."

"He had a really, really big dream. He thought that if he could teach other Spiders about how we lived up here, maybe he could build his own community, with his own kind. He felt that there was no reason why, Spiders couldn't also have a better, more harmonious life, by working together."

"But he was way too scared of heights to climb down, and he way was too big to carry safely. As you are now Blinky. He tried the vents a couple of times, but always popped up a few days later on another part of the rooftop."

"Please don't climb down there Blinky!" Steve pleaded with a panicked look on his face.

"Crossing the road is suicide for a spider, your friend Bill really did save your life by carrying you over it last time."

Blinky slumped back down against his favourite pipe, and sighed.

"So unless I magically turn into a bird, I'm stuck up here, just like here was!"

"Fraid so," said Dave.

"Yup, best to make the most of it," added Steve.

Franky just nodded.

Chapter 13
Hot Potatoes

Another two weeks had passed, it was quickly apparent that a very hot summer was brewing. The heat was almost unbearable, even before the Suns face was in full view.

It seemed to be getting hotter by the day, and as the Sun blazed overhead, it had so much power, that Blinky had to spend most of the day sleeping in the shade.

Ironically, his air conditioning box was blisteringly hot in the Sun. But luckily, he found plenty of cool dark cubby holes to chill in during the hottest hours. He only usually came out in the much cooler evenings, after sitting and watching the sunset alone, as usual.

He would look out over the river to the distant park, trying to imagine what exciting things might be happening down there right now. His daydreams always featured the biggest, and very tallest tree in the far away patch of green.

Although Blinky, had now kind of accepted his fate. He did realise that as far as the fate of a spider goes, this must be one of the most fortunate ever. He had everything he could possibly want. Food, shelter, safety, friends. Why on Earth did he feel such an urge, to leave it all behind?

He was gently drifting into such a day dream, one hot summers afternoon. When he heard the day shift coming back, they were quite a bit earlier than usual. He thought nothing of it, until there was a sudden agonised scream on the rooftop, followed by a lot of flapping and laughter.

Blinky rushed out to investigate, but as he climbed up onto the ledge, all he could hear was, "Shhh Shhhhhh Shhhhh Shhhhh."

There was Dave, Steve and Franky, all standing in a line smiling at him.

"What's going on lads?" He asked. "Was that Cid screaming?...... Is he OK?"

"Ohhhhh, Cid..... Yeh, he ummmmm.... he errrrrrr.... He banged his toe! Ouchy! Don't you just hate it when then happens?" Dave lifted his foot and pointed at it.

"My face always goes that red when I do it too," he added quickly. Trying to justify Cids' glowing red cheeks.

"Banged it a goodun, didn't you Cid?"

"Alright now though, isn't it mate?"

"Nothing a good rub won't fix, eh Cid." Said Dave without taking his eyes off Blinky, in fact everyone was looking at him.

Blinky had experienced having so much attention on him before, he recognised how uncomfortable it made him feel. So he immediately knew, something was going on.

Dave was clearly lying, but to find out why, and before this story can go any further, I must tell you the truth about what really happened to Cid.

While out on the day shift earlier, Dave was down in the now infamous park. He was scouting for something of interest, when he happened across a nearly full packet of crisps.

Nobody was around, so he went down for a better look, and a taste test of course. The tortilla triangles he had found were of the extra, extra spicy variety. The bag even had a picture with three chillis on it.

With one taste, Daves' beak was on fire!

After a few minutes of flapping around in circles, with tears streaming from his eyes, the fierce burning sensation gradually subsided.

This was by far the most wicked snack Dave had ever put in his beak! One thing was obvious, this was the hottest joke that had come Daves way for years, and he fully intended to milk it for as much fun as he possibly could.

One by one, Dave guided the rest of the day shift to the prize with a surprise. He sat laughing in a tree, as they caught their first taste of the cripplingly hot crisps.

This may sound a bit mean, but really, it was classic Pigeon humour at its absolute best.

All the Pigeons found it totally hilarious, after the pain had subsided of course. They then hid quietly behind a park bench, eagerly waiting for Dave to put on another performance. He would pretend that he was leading them to something far less exciting than crisps, often just stale bread. The art was in convincing the victim that he had only just seen the Tortillas, and wanted to get them first.

They all fell for it, racing in to be the first to get a taste, pleasing Dave tremendously. Well all of them except Franky, for a start he's not easily excited. Plus, he knows Daves bad acting far too well to fall for one of his traps.

It had been so much fun, that they took as many as they could carry up to the others on the roof. This joke was just too good to wait for the end of the shift.

Back on the roof top. It was Cid that was the first to fall into the tortilla trap, as it later became known. But he had made such a loud fuss about it, that everyone else on the rooftop now knew it was a trick.

Blinky however, had been in his box all along, and there was a slight chance he might take the bait.

So this was the reason for the uncomfortable edge, that now hung in the atmosphere across the roof. It was so heavy that Blinky could almost touch it, yet still he remained clue less as to its cause.

Eventually, it was Steve who broke the tension as the trap sprang into action. With one smooth move, he swung a whole crisp out from behind his back.

"Look what treat I've got for you." He said, hopping forward and offering Blinky the big tortilla triangle.

It was in that moment, Dave noticed the bright Orange wind sock on a nearby buildings helipad pick up suddenly. This was the secret behind Daves legendarily accurate weather forecasts.

Just as Steve passed the crisp to Blinky, Dave turned and said. "I think the winds going to pick up."

Blinkys' knees bent under the weight, as he disappeared underneath the crisp. It was so big, that he could only just hold it up with four of his feet.

Just then, the tall dish on their skyscrapers communications tower, started to squeak and rattle, as it only did when the strongest of winds hit it.

Blinky only had enough time to give Steve a quick fear filled glance, before the gust rolled in!

Whoooooooosh!

In less than a Blinkys blink, he was swept several metres away from the building. With nothing around him but thin air, Blinky held tight onto the only thing he could. The Tortilla!

To his surprise, he wasn't falling as fast as he had expected. The fact was, the aerodynamic shape of the crisp made for an excellent glider. Blinky discovered that by pulling down on either side, he could even steer the snack to a certain degree.

It felt a bit like being on Bills back again, but this time he was in control. It was then that Blinky knew exactly which way to steer his delicious chilli delta wing.

So he pulled the peak of his tasty glider around, aiming it straight at the distant park he had dreamed of seeing for so long.

"I hope I can make it...... No I believe I can make it!"

"There's no turning back now, I have to make it!"

As he crossed the cooler air rising from the river, the temperature drop caused him to lose height much quicker than before. It was soon obvious, he was going fall well short of his target.

Blinky closed his eyes saying, "Nooooooo Noooooo," to himself in despair. When a pair of voices rang out in stereo on either side of him.

"Need a lift mate?"

It was Steve and Dave, and despite the dire situation, they couldn't help but have a giggle at their own joke.

Steve shouted across. "If this goes wrong, it was all Frankys idea, ok?"

At that, the two Pigeons rolled over and beat their wings simultaneously towards the underneath of the glider.

WHOOOOOOMPH!

The upward force was enough to give Blinky a short burst of lift, so they followed him, and repeated the move as often as they could.

It was beginning to look hopeful again, with a couple more wing beats, he might just make it all the way to the tree.

WHOOOOOOOMPH........ WHOOOOOOOMPH

There, that was it, he was right on target now!

Blinkys moment of relief was short lived though, as he realised he was travelling at quite some pace. He had been so focused on reaching the tree, he hadn't given any thought to exactly how he was going to stop when he got there.

As the huge oak tree came rushing towards him, there really wasn't much Blinky could do except brace himself for the impact.

With his front legs occupied clinging onto the crisp, he could do nothing to block the thick wall of leaves racing at his face.

So, he blinked at what could have been his last ever blinkworthy view, taking it in from every angle right up until the last possible moment.

At the last second, Blinky squeezed all of his eyes shut as tight as he could, Letting out a defiant battle cry just before impact.

"YeeeearrrRRrrRRRrrrRRr.........

SLAP! "OW"

SLAP! SLAP! "OW, OW."

Blinky opened one eye to have a quick look to see if it was over, it wasn't.

SLAP! "OW!" Right in the eye!

Chapter 14
A Fresh Start

It had been a while since the last leaf had slapped Blinky in the face. So he braved another tentative glance, with his remaining good eyes.

The sight that slowly came into focus was absolutely magical, the interior of the tree really was a bewitching sight to behold.

The massive trunk, as it rose up from the distant grass below. It had branches like thick wide arms, outstretched, holding on to its vast green veil of leaves.

The tree was so efficient at harvesting sunlight, that at this time of year it was rare for even a single ray to pass all the way through the canopy. The leaf filtered light, bathed the inside of the tree in a rich, warm green glow.

Even though being repeatedly spanked in the face by leaves, was quite a painful experience.

Blinky was soon very grateful for them, the multiple impacts had slowed him down to a rather graceful drift.

He was just starting to get the hang of controlling the glider, and managed to line himself up with a nice thick, long horizontal branch. He prepared to make his landing.

As he slowly got lower, and his feet were a just a legs length above the branch. He let go of the crisp, dropping rather skillfully onto the bark runway. Incredibly, he landed perfectly on all eight legs.

The extra spicy tortilla however, was not so fortunate! It sailed on, crashing straight into the trees trunk and shattering into three scrumptious pieces. One of the yummy shards pinged off the edge of the branch, making the one way journey into the void below.

Blinky brushed himself off, and was in the middle of taking a deep sigh of relief. When out of nowhere, came a very excited high pitched voice.

"Wow mister, that was epic! You take kite flying to a whole new level!"

Blinky jumped in surprise. "Ooooooh little Spiderling, I didn't see you there!"

"Sorry Sir," squeaked the Spiderling bashfully.

"But you're just amazing, wait until I tell the others about this."

Others, thought Blinky to himself.

"What's your name mister? I'm still just plain old spider. I haven't found my name yet, have you found yours? If not, I'd call you Kite. But of course, I bet an amazing Spider like you already has a wicked name, huh?"

Blinky had a brain wave. Not only did he have the chance to change his name, and have a fresh start. But also the opportunity to give this excitable young Spiderling, the honour of giving it to him.

It was considered a proud achievement, to give another Spider their name. Blinky could see such hope in the youngsters eyes, it seemed like a win win situation.

"Thank you Spider," said Blinky. "I've been waiting for someone to find a name for me all this time, and Kite it is!"

Blinky looked down and winked at the youngster affectionately, who obviously being in a name giving mood, then said. "Or Winky, or, or Winker? That could be your name too if you like?"

"NO NO!" Fired Blinky quickly. "Kite is perfect."

"Thank you again. I hope that one day I can return the favour, and find just as great a name for you!"

Spider gestured with his little leg towards the tree trunk. "This way," he said hopping off down the branch in a kind of odd skip. But mind you, it is hard not to look a bit strange skipping, when you've got eight legs.

Spider then disappeared underneath the branch where it met the trunk, and repeated loudly. "This way."

Blinky, who is now called Kite, followed obediently. He was quietly curious where the Spiderling was taking him, and he couldn't help but wonder who the others were.

He didn't have to wait long to find out, as Spider slipped through a big knot in the trees trunk, disappearing into the darkness. Young Spiders reassuring voice echoed out of the foreboding void in the tree. "THIS WAY, this way, this way. OOOOH, ooooh, ooooh. ECHO, echo, echo."

Kite ventured through the black hole in the tree trunk, soon emerging into a big warm green circle. The tree top was completely hollow, and light was flooding down from above through a jagged opening. Long ago a lightening strike had zapped the top off, exposing the solid looking tree trunk, as no more than an empty shell.

Blinkys' gaze was snapped back from the hole above, when he noticed another big Spider out of the corner of his eye. There, a very brightly coloured female spider stood, frozen, like a statue, staring straight at him.

She was clearly in the middle of doing something, and had still paused mid motion at the sight of another spider.

The pause didn't last long though, her instincts kicked in and she quickly turned to face him, taking up a very aggressive stance.

This was understandable behaviour, as she was standing in front of a huge ball of silk. It looked like it had only recently hatched, and it was absolutely covered in Spiderlings.

Suddenly, Kite was overcome by the familiar paralysing effect, of having a multitude of eyes focused on him. Once again, his words failed him, and the female was becoming increasingly anxious.

She looked as though she was just about to strike, when a little voice piped up breaking the silence.

"Everyone, this is my new friend Kite!"

"I gave him his name, literally just now." Said Spider, taking a short bow.

"I called him Kite, because.... Well he flies just like one. You should have seen it, it was extreme!"

"You can fly?" Asked the female doubtfully.

"Well, errrrrrr."

"I could, but my errrrrmmm, crisp, is broken now....... So I can't fly anymore."

Kite was tripping all over his words, desperately struggling to think straight with all those little eyes and faces looking up at him.

It was his bold little friend, that came to to his rescue once again.

"Yes, it's true. He crashed his errrr.... Crisp?" Spider said, looking to Kite for confirmation that they were talking about the same thing.

Kite finally pulled himself together, as he realised he was no longer Blinky, he was Kite now!

He spoke clearly, precisely, and with the confidence that he had genuinely earned on his dramatic journey so far.

He also realised, that he now had a name that belonged to a fearless and brave kind of Spider. One which he was determined to live up to, from now on.

"Yes, I flew my extra spicy crisp glider." He started, flashing young Spider a cheeky smile.

I flew all the way here from the very top, of the very tallest building."

I have come here looking for a new life, hopefully one a little calmer, and less exciting than it has been so far."

"Oh, I see." Said the female, relaxing a little bit."

Blinky was absolutely mesmerised, by the trio of striking yellow stripes on her back. He had no idea Spiders could be so colourful.

"I am sorry to have to tell you Kite, that place can not be here!"

"But why?" Asked Kite. "This place is so nice."

"The only thing I can think of, is that it's a bit exposed here, hungry birds could easily get in through there." He looked up at the big hole above them.

"No Kite, the birds don't come near this tree. Not anymore!"

"Look..... Listen......"

"Near or far, no bird has been seen, or heard from close to this tree, for many moons now."

"There is a great evil here!"

A Monster that lurks below!"

Although he was listening. Kite had also been trying to find a way of leaning against the tree trunk, in the kind of casual way he thought someone with a name like Kite would.

But it didn't matter how cool he looked, as soon as she said Monster, Blinky was back!

It was a quick eye wobble, more like a twitch, maybe nobody had noticed.

"A Mmmm mmm mmmmMonster you say?" Blinky spluttered eventually.

The Spiderlings all giggled.

She gave them a stern glare, instantly restoring silence!

"All have gone, all except us. But as soon as the Spiderlings are old enough, we will follow them to the safety of the long grasses."

"As it happens, I was just about to tell the Spiderlings the story of the monster. Let's see if they are still giggling then!"

"Make yourself comfortable Kite. By the way, my name is Aura, and you are more than welcome to come with us, when we leave this tree in a few days. For as you will soon see, it is not safe to stay here."

Kite slid casually down the tree trunk, and into a sitting position. He was trying to be as smooth as he could be, whilst gripped with fear. Unfortunately the tree bark scratched his back on the way down, making him yelp out loud.

"Thank YOWWWWWWCH!"

The Spiderlings all giggled again.

"You, I meant thank you." He said looking down at his now crossed legs, which made him resemble a dark brown knot.

In fact, the name Knot is a very common one amongst Spiders. This is due to complications they encounter, the first time they try sitting down as youngsters.

Chapter 15
A monster in our midst

When everyone had finally settled, Aura began her story.

"I was born and raised in this tree, for many generations my ancestors have used it, as a safe place to raise their Spiderlings"

"I was about to start my first family here, that means you lot." She said, pointing at her vast hoard. "You were already wrapped up here in this ball of silk, so I had no choice but to stay behind."

"The memory of that day, is as clear to me now, as it ever was, or ever shall be."

"I was out on the branch practising my hunting skills, when I found a broken twig. The twig would wobble about when I walked on it, and I was seeing how long I could keep my balance. Suddenly, a big Sparrow swooped in and picked up the twig, with me still sitting on it!"

Everyone took a deep breath!

"The Bird carried me high up into the tree top, and dropped me into the nest it was building. Luckily, my colours blended nicely with all the old twigs and moss in the nest. I knew that as long as I didn't move, I might be able to remain un-noticed until a chance came to escape.

"At the birds first glance away, I snuck to the underside of the nest and out of sight. There I stayed, motionless, waiting for the right time to make a break for it."

"The Sparrow busied itself around the nest, arranging, and then re-arranging the twigs until they were perfect. It was starting to get dark, it was that funny time of day when the light starts to give way to the night."

"But even in the twilight glow, there was no denying what I saw huddled within a deep knot in the tree trunk. Just its front legs were showing, but there was no doubt what so ever."

"It was an absolutely, enormous, Spider!"

"As I was staring at those huge legs, unable to move a muscle, or avert my gaze. I started to wonder if I was seeing things. But then I saw a red tinge flash across its knees, as the last rays of the retreating Sun shimmered over it's big hairy legs."

"And then!"

"He STRUCK!"

"The giant Spider sprung out of its hiding spot with incredible speed."

"Before the Sparrow knew what was happening, the massive Red Knee Tarantula had wrestled the increasingly terrified Bird into its deadly embrace. The Sparrow was still completely clue less as to exactly what was going on, that is until the Tarantula administered its paralysing bite.

Within seconds, the Birds claws went "QUITCHHH." Locking into a clenched position, as the poison rapidly took hold."

Auras entire audience went. "EEEEEEEEK." Including the cool and ever so brave Kite.

"I knew that might be my only chance to escape, so I took it. I crept as quietly and quickly back to the others as I could. But when I got back, of course nobody believed me!"

"For not even in the ancient Spider chronicles, were there spiders even one third the size of a Sparrow!"

My mother said to me, "A Spider having a bird for dinner, that's impossible dear. My what an imagination you young Spiderlings have."

"Never the less, I knew what I had seen. There was certainly no way I was going to sleep that night, or any other from then on!"

"I kept a sharp eye out every night afterwards, only sleeping during the day, when there were lots of other eyes to keep watch for the beast."

"Even now, I stay on guard all night, stealing an afternoon nap whenever I can."

"It was on the fifth night, that I found the courage to venture out to the borders of the branches. I like to sit alone, and look through the leaves at the moonlight. My absolute favourite thing, is gazing at the beautiful glow of that Silvery White disc, as it wanders across the night sky."

"That evening, I happened to look down across the moonlit grass, I saw a huge shadow scurrying away from the base of our tree. I only saw it for a second as it slipped off into the night, but It had the unmistakable movement of a gargantuant Spider in a hurry!"

"I rushed to wake the others, but they still didn't believe me. Eventually I managed to get two of my brothers to come and keep watch with me. I promised to make sure that nobody in the whole tree got any sleep if they didn't."

"The three us stood guard on the branch, watching and waiting. The park always looked so beautiful as the trees danced gently with the breeze, draped in capes of moonlight. But there was no time to enjoy it this time, after all, there WAS a monster around."

"It was in these last few moments of light, a shadow wobbled clumsily, but quickly across the grass. It was heading straight towards our tree!"

"Luckily, this time the others saw it too! Even though they found it hard to believe, none of them could deny what they had seen."

"It was undoubtedly a spider of immense size, and it was now somewhere in our tree!"

"Once the word got round the branches that the monster was real, everyone was terrified. They quickly planned to evacuate the tree, as soon as Spiderly possible."

"But I had to stay, you lot were already growing, and starting to move. There was no way I was going to leave you behind to be born alone, defenceless and completely oblivious to the danger that lurked in the shadows below."

"And so now, here we are, counting the days until we can all escape this terrible menace together."

Kite and the Spiderlings were all dumbstruck, and just about to explode into an exited chatter, when the most terrifying sound came blaring up from below them.

"ROOOOOOOAAAAAAAARRRRRRRRR-OWWAAAAAAAAA!"

The monstrous bellow that bounced up from the depths, made the Spiderlings, and even the brave Kite scatter in fear.

Aura looked to Kite, searching for some reassurance. Her face was stricken with fear, but Kite was finding it more and more impossible to act cool. He desperately tried to think, how would a hero like Kite react right now.

Just then, another very different noise echoed up from the depths.

"MMMMMMMMMMMMMMMM YUMYUMYUM!"

"That can only be, HIM!" Squealed Aura. "Maybe he's coming for us right NOW?"

Kite was in another desperate situation, and for a moment, completely forgot he was trying so hard to be as cool as Kite.

Luckily without the focus required to keep up his fake persona, he began to think clearly again.

"We need to get out of here, that's for sure. It's very exposed, and we would be too easily trapped. If he really is as big as you say, we should go to the thinner branches at the edge of the tree. They might not take his weight, and we'd have lots of escape routes."

Aura was a bit taken aback by his confidence, and sound logic. "Great plan Kite." She said, smiling at him for the first time.

So they all streamed down the long branch that Kite had used earlier as a runway, heading out to the furthest edge of the trees wide reach.

As the Spiderlings marched obediently passed in a seemingly endless line, Kite noticed his broken glider. It was still sitting there in pieces, over by the tree trunk.

He went and picked up a piece, signalling to Aura to come over.

"This is what's left of my glider." Kite put the two pieces together and held them up.

"There's a bit missing," Aura said, pointing at the big gap in the corner.

"So there is," said Blinky. "I jumped off just before it crashed into the tree trunk, the other piece must have fallen off the branch." Kite leaned gingerly over the edge, trying to see what path the crisp may have taken.

"It's a type of human food, I must say they actually have some pretty tasty stuff, especially cookies, Mmmmmmm." Kites eyes almost closed, as he remembered the scrumptious experience of having a double chop chip cookie slowly dissolving in his mouth.

"This, is a Tortilla, and apparently it's extra extra spicy, whatever that means. I haven't tasted it, but apparently it's like having a fire in your mouth. A hot one too, if the colour of Cids' face was anything to judge by."

"Who is Cid?" Asked Aura.

Kite couldn't help but chuckle a bit, as he remembered how funny the Pigeons were.

"Cid is my one of my friends, he's a Pigeon that lives up on the top of the skyscraper. And the only creature I've seen actually eat one of these hot crisps. I'll tell you the story later, it's a good one."

Luckily for me, they also fly pretty well. Otherwise I would have dropped like a stone off that skyscraper, and I never would have made it all the way here."

Aura was staring at him, but in a fascinated way. I think it's your turn to tell the next story Kite!"

"Absolutely, I must say it has been a bit of a mad one so far. If we make it through this, I'll tell you all about it."

Kite was still giggling a bit to himself, thinking about how Cid had screamed when he tasted the crisp.

Then the penny dropped!

Kite stopped mid step. "It was the crisp!"

"The crisp?" Repeated Aura with a quizzical look on her face.

"Yes, yes, that's it! The missing piece of the crisp! It fell down there, and the beast must have found it."

"You may well be right Kite, but what difference does it make?" Aura asked.

"The difference is, I'm pretty sure he liked it!"

"Aura, there's something I have to do. Wait for me at the branches edge, but if I'm not back by sunrise, then leave without me. You must leave immediately for the grasslands to find your kin, leave at daybreak, you must promise!"

"Wait Kite, what are you going to do? Don't leave."

"I reckon that he not only liked, but loved my tortilla. If that is the case, then these other two pieces should be at least enough to buy me an audience with the beast. Maybe even enough to bargain for our safety here."

"But what if he eats you?" Cried Aura

"Yes, well. There is that."

"But I don't think he will."

"Trust me! I've got a plan.

"kind of!"

Chapter 16
A Risky Move

With no more words, just a lingering look of worry from Aura. Kite turned, and with the two remaining pieces of the crisp held out on either side of him, he fastened a strong line to the branch, and dramatically launched himself backwards. Down, down, into the darkness he dropped, deep towards the very heart of the old Oak tree he fell.

He was actually rather pleased with his dismount from the branch, he imagined it looked rather impressive, and very Kite like!

But as he descended further and further from that moment, it sunk in just how fearful the moment he was fast approaching was.

What would Kite do? What would Kite do? He kept repeating in his head over and over, as he reeled himself out lower and lower. Down he dropped, eventually reaching an impassable barrier of branches, that dominated the view beneath him.

When his feet finally touched the first branch, he was immediately faced with a huge dark opening, that led into the deep caverns hidden within the tree.

It was then that something occurred to him, unexpectedly, and totally out of the blue. There he stood, on the precipice of the most terrifying moment imaginable. Motionless, facing the void of terror, just thinking to himself.

"I don't know what Kite would do, because I'm not Kite!"

"I am Blinky!"

It was Blinky that saved me all those times, not Kite!

So what would Blinky do???

"Right," He said to himself quietly.

"Go in, say hello. If it all goes wrong, chuck the crisp at him and leg it!"

And so there it was! With a faultlessly simple plan in place, Blinky courageously went forth into the lair of the Tarantula.

As he passed through the jagged edge of a huge, gnarled wooden gateway, Blinkys eyes slowly adjusted to the loss of light. A long dark passage gradually unveiled itself from the gloom, it sloped down into the main trunk, and into absolute darkness. Blinkys heart was beginning to race, and his Blink started kicking in again.

As he stepped into the blackness, he felt a very familiar feeling underfoot. It was web, but this time it was, an incredibly thick web.

So, with the foundation of his fears thoroughly solidified, and panic on the verge of setting in at any given moment. He bravely carried on, down the industrial carpet of heavy web, and into the inner core of the trunk.

The tension was suddenly and sharply shattered, by a very loud voice coming from the darkness beyond!

"AAAAAAAAAAAAAAHHHHHHHHHHHHHHHH HHHHHH!!!!!!!!!!!!"

It was a proper scream!

The scream was so loud that Blinky had to cover his ears. The spicy tortilla pieces proving their diversity once again, making pretty effective ear plugs.

"What you doing in here?"

The voice came booming from a shuffling dark mass, curled up tight in the corner.

"I'm errrrrrrr Blinky, hello. Please don't eat me, I brought you a present." Blinky said nervously.

"Wait outside will you?" Bellowed the voice.

"It's bad enough you had to wake me up from a luuuuuuverly dream, but now you're just going to stand there staring at me. How rude!"

"Oh, errrrrr, yes of course, sorry."

Blinky backed slowly out onto the branch, making sure he had at least a couple of escape routes in mind, just in case.

After a couple of minutes had passed, four thick furry legs came into view, all with Red stripes on their knees.

Then a huge head covered in big black eyes came looming out of the shadows.

"Sorry about that Blinky, I'm always a bit grumpy when I wake up." The massive spider said through a deep yawn.

"Bit pointless though, being grumpy when you're on your own, It is nice to have someone else to be grumpy with for a change.

"Aaaaaaand, you've brought a present! How exciting!"

The Tarantula finally introduced himself. "I'm Eric, Eric the Red! I'm named after a great Viking leader."

"Wow," Said Blinky. "I don't even know what a Viking is, but that sounds pretty impressive, and it certainly suits a magnificent spider like you!"

Eric sighed. "Of course, you're a wild spider, why would you know anything about the Vikings. I've spent nearly all of my life stuck in a glass box, with nothing to look at except a wide screen TV that never seemed to be turned off.

My human was a bit lazy, eventually he started completely forgetting to buy me food. The times when he did remember me, he would just chuck in a bit of whatever he was having.

Fried chicken, pizza, crisps, even half a bar of chocolate once!"

"It was absolutely delicious though, human food is amazing!"

"Quite often he would forget to close the lid on my box, so I used to sneak out and change the channel on the TV. He had no idea that while he was fast asleep, I would sit up on his shoulder, watching documentaries while dipping my legs into his ice cream."

"I must admit, I did have a good life there, I had everything I needed. I saw so many amazing and beautiful things, you can't even begin to imagine. But I only ever saw them through the screen of a television."

"I so desperately wanted to see some of it, even if it was just a little piece."

"So one warm night, when he left the lid of my box and the window, both wide open. I took my chance. and made a run for the park. Eventually ending up here, in this very tree."

"The first few nights were brilliant, I found this great hollow tree to keep me warm and hidden. I would run around the park all night long, just stretching my legs and picking up whatever food the humans left behind."

"But I don't always find something to eat, days could go by without any dinner at all. There was a Human that came every day just before dark, he would empty the bins and clear all the scraps from the floor.

Occasionally I would get so desperately hungry, but it was far too dangerous to go down into the park during the day. I had no choice sometimes, but to look up into the tree for food."

"So you really did eat a Sparrow?" Asked Blinky

The rest of Eric slowly spilled out from the hole in the tree. He reared up on to his hind legs, and stretched himself out onto the branch above, showing just how truly massive he really was.

Eric yawned again as he stretched.

"Yep, I did. But he had it coming!"

"The noise he would make, just as I was getting ready for bed. EVVVVVERY DAY!"

"So after a couple of nights without any luck in the bins. I was sitting there, starving, with a rumbling empty stomach."

"And then him!"

"Tweet tweet tweet!"

"And then, Tweet tweet tweet!"

"Guess what came next! Yep, you got it. Tweet.... Tweet... Terrr-weet...!"

"Eventually, I completely lost it. I had no choice but to go Jungle style on him!"

"Big meal that was! And afterwards, with a full belly and nothing but peace and quiet. I had the best days sleep, ever!"

Eric tucked his legs back in, as he settled back down facing Blinky.

"Well," He said. "By the way you've been looking at me for the last few minutes, I can see why you're called Blinky."

Eric started to laugh, "I have to say, that is actually pretty funny."

"And is that my present you've got behind your back?"

"Oh yes," Said Blinky, whipping out the remaining tortilla shards from behind his back.

"Ooooohhhh," said Eric. "Is that the same as the one that fell from the sky earlier? I was grumpy with that too, but only for a few moments."

"You are full of surprises aren't you little spider." Said Eric, as he took a big bite. "Yeeeeeeeeooooooooooohhhhhhhh-hOWWWWW."

"Ooooohhhh, MMMMMM, Mumph Mumph Mumph."

"That is human food at its very, VERY best."

Blinky could only watch, as the monstrous Spider slipped a corner into his mouth. He sucked it slowly with his eyes closed, only chewing it after the mouth tingling spices had dissipated.

"So, do tell Blinky, what exactly is it that brings you into the lair of the terrifying Treeantula?"

Eric made himself comfortable, slowly licking the intense spices off the crisp. He was pulling all kinds of interesting faces, each time his tongue touched it.

"Well." Started Blinky.

"I came here looking for a new home, just as you did."

"But I believe, that if we all worked together, it could be so much more than that. It could be a community!"

Eric stopped munching and leant forward, he gave Blinky an intrigued sideways glance.

"Well, you've certainly got my attention little fella, but how on earth do you intend to make that happen?"

"There are a thousand terrified young orb weavers, hiding with their mother, up in the branches above us right now. There's me, and there's you. That's a start at least, isn't it?"

"If I could guarantee their safety, by making sure you always have plenty of human food. Then we can all stay here, and maybe build something really special!"

Eric was thoroughly enthralled. "Sounds great Blinky, I'm not going to be stuffing my face with any Orb Weaver Spiderlings anytime soon. So nobody needs to worry about that one, okey dokey?"

"But what's your plan to get the human food here?"

Blinky turned, and looking out through a gap in the lower branches, he said.

"I have friends in high places!"

"They were always talking about how much food there is, so much so, that they have to leave lots behind. If we could convince them to drop some off here at the tree, I'm sure there would be enough for all of us."

"Who is they?" Quizzed Eric.

"Yes, that's it," said Blinky, almost shouting with excitement. "The Pigeons will help, I'm sure!"

"Pigeons?" Repeated a confused Eric.

"Eric, if you're in, meet me tomorrow in the hollow at the very top of the tree trunk."

"Oh I'm soooooo up for an adventure," said Eric. This has to be the most exciting thing that's happened to me. Well, at least since that time I snuck out of my box during a house party. I hid in the drinks cabinet, waiting for the perfect moment."

Eric couldn't help but laugh at the memory of that evening. The panicked guests after they realised there was a Tarantula on the loose, then when poor old Doris pulled a bottle out of the cabinet, and there was Eric, perched on top, legs up and bearing his fangs.

"Absolute classic." Eric said to himself.

"You had probably better warn the others I'm coming though, it will be a bit of a shock if they're not expecting me."

Unfortunately though, the Pigeons sense of humour had rubbed off on Blinky more than he had realised. Which made it very hard to resist the chance of a gag, especially one as good as this.

"Welllllllll, there's no harm in you making a bit of an entrance."

Blinky gave Eric a cheeky quadruple wink. Then climbed back onto his Silk line, and hauled himself up to the branches above.

Chapter 17
Revelations

Aura, and the Spiderlings, were all very relieved to see Blinky returning safely. He was quick to reassure them, that they were now safe in the tree. He led them promptly back to the warm tree hollow, where they all bedded down for the night. After Blinkys confident reassurance, even Aura had a full nights sleep, for the first time in ages.

Blinky had a much needed, long and deep sleep, but was rudely woken by the distant sound of someone calling his name.

"Bliiiinnnnkyyyyy, Bliiiiiiinnnnnnkyyyyyy." Came the faint voice from afar.

As Blinky snapped from his slumber. There was that initial confusion you get, when waking up in a new place for the first time. His focus slowly tuned in on Auras puzzled face, she was quite close, and staring straight at him.

"Kite, there's some bird flying around out there, just beyond the leaves. It sounds like it's calling out a name. I think it keeps shouting, Blinky?"

Blinky instantly sprung out of bed and up on to his feet, shouting excitedly. "It must be one of my winged friends!" He ran out onto the branches as quickly as he could.

"DOWN HERE!" He yelled.

"DOOOOOOWWWWWNNNNN HEEEEEEEERRRRREEEEEE!"

But Blinkys little voice wasn't anywhere near loud enough. "It's no good, he can't hear me."

Blinky thought for a moment, then an idea popped into his head.

"Right everyone! Spiderlings, Aura. I want you all to shout, DOWN HERE, as loud as you can, when I count to three."

"But, it has to be all at exactly the same time, OK?"

"One, two, three.... "DOOOOOWWWWWNNNN HEEERRRRRRREEEEE!" They all shouted together!

It was only Blinky that wasn't surprised by the volume of their unanimous shout. The sheer power when all their voices joined forces, would always be a shock the first time you heard it.

There was a short silence, as all the Spiderlings looked at each other, stunned by the monstrous noise they had just made. Then, after a few seconds, the leaves at the outer canopy rustled, as if to answer their call.

All eyes tried to track the sound as it came closer, then suddenly, crashing through the leaves came, a Big Blue Tit!

"BILL!" Shouted Blinky.

Billingsworth Blue Tit the 3rd, was coming in to land. He lined himself up perfectly down the branch, and headed straight at the mass of terrified Spiderlings.

Bill was planning a spectacular landing to introduce himself, and he certainly managed that, even if it wasn't quite what he had in mind!

He was just about to spin into a drop flutter, which was his favourite move for showing off in front of an audience, when suddenly!

Eric the Red reared up onto the top of the crooked tree trunk, he lifted his front legs up in an attacking posture, and cheerfully said.

"Morning all."

Bill completely freaked out mid landing, and it went horribly, horribly wrong. He came down mid spin awkwardly, crashing in a brightly coloured heap in front of the Spiderlings

To which they all went, "OooooooH!"

They then turned to say good morning, to whoever it was behind them, bidding them such a pleasant greeting.

"Morning, AAAAAAAHHHHHHHH!"

Eric towered over all of them, the shadow of just one of his legs was enough to put all the Spiderlings into darkness.

Aura passed out cold on the spot, and the Spiderlings didn't know which way to run. They kept bumping into each other, in a panicked disorder.

They eventually decided to take their chances behind the big clumsy bird, and scrambled frantically in behind Bill, who was only just picking himself up off the branch.

Luckily, Eric quickly diffused the situation with a proper introduction. But that didn't help poor Aura, who was still thoroughly decked.

By the time she finally came round, everyone except her had been introduced. Bill and Eric were already chatting like old friends, and the Spiderlings were climbing all over Eric, in pure amazement at just how huge he was.

Blinky was by her side when she woke. "Ahhh there you are, welcome back, how are you feeling?"

Eric leaned in saying. "Hi, I'm Eric. Sorry I gave you a fright, it was actually all Blinkys idea!"

Then Bill leaned in from the other side. "Hiiiiiiiii, I'm Bill. I was actually trying to give everyone a fright with a daring landing. But when Eric pulled his stunt, it was me that ended up scared. Pretty rapid Karma huh!"

Aura slowly sat up, again with a confused look on her face. "Kite, why do they all keep calling you Blinky?"

Bill was the first to crease up, "Pahahahahahaaaahahahahaaaa. KITE. Phahahahahahahahaaaaaa."

Bills laugh was as infectious as ever, and soon everyone was sniggering along with him. Everyone that is, except for Blinky.

Bill continued talking through his laughter. "He tried telling me his name was Warrior when I first met him, Hahahahahahaaaaaa"

"Alright Bill, that's enough," said Blinky frowning. "Aura, please allow me to explain."

"When I first got here, I did actually already have a name, thanks to Bill here." Bill Bowed graciously.

"The thing is, I really didn't like it at all, and little Spider gave me the chance to change it to something I did like. You see, in all the legends and epic tales, the heroes always have great names. Not silly names like Blinky!"

"I guess, I just always wanted to be a hero. But I didn't think that would be possible, not with an awful name like Blinky."

"But you know what, I've realised something since then, it was me that made it all this way. It had absolutely nothing to do with my name, not one bit. In fact, the truth is, that if I had been Kite all along, I would probably have perished long before making it here."

"It was actually, my funny blink that has saved me so many times on this journey. Without it I probably would not be right here, right now, with all of you."

"So from now on, I will be Blinky! And I shall proudly wear the name, that has led me to this monumental moment. It was Blinky that brought you all together here, as we balance precariously on the precipice of a new beginning."

To Blinkys surprise, Aura started to giggle.

"What's so funny?" He asked her.

"It's just that, well, the Spiderlings have been calling you Blinky, ever since you left last night.

Because of the, you know, the eye thing you do."

Blinky couldn't help but to crack a smile, and a giggle along with everyone else.

Bill was not only impressed by Blinkys little speech, but also very intrigued by his final statement.

"So, what exactly is going on here Blinky? The Pigeons filled me in on the many stories from the skyscraper, did you really fly a crisp all the way here?"

Blinky nodded to Bill, and then little Spider jumped up shouting "Yep he did, I saw the landing, it was amazing!"

"You certainly have had an exciting life so far haven't you, and in such a short space of time. My how much you have grown since we first met, and not just in size."

"I can't wait to hear all about this new beginning you're talking about?"

Blinky was quite moved by Bills words, he carefully unravelled the details of his idea to everyone. He described in great detail his final goal, drawing a vivid picture with words, of the Tree of Silk.

"Well." Said Bill.

"That's a pretty impressive dream you've got there Blinky, how on earth did you think that up?"

Blinky indulged him, along with his now captivated audience, by recounting his tale up until now. He told of how he would sit alone in his box, high up on top of the skyscraper. Looking down at this tree in particular, as it stood distinctively out, in the distant park.

How he would think about Bongos dream of uniting the Spiders, and how Bongo thought he could have made their lives better. He described how he would often sit alone, looking out over the city far below. Also dreaming of how if he only had the chance, he could use all that he had learned from the Pigeons, to make a real positive difference.

Blinky went on to explain, that it was in that moment he had decided. If he ever managed to find his way to this tree, he would do his absolute best, to fulfil Bongos' incredibly noble dream.

Nobody spoke, they all just sat staring at Blinky. Of course, they didn't realise how uncomfortable that made him feel. But for once, it didn't really bother him.

Eric broke the silence, by starting to cheer and clap wildly, which was followed by a standing ovation from the others.

"You really are an amazing little Spider Blinky," Bill said. "I think it's a wonderful idea, and I'll do whatever I can, to help you make it a reality!"

"Thank you all, really. But I can't do this without the help of every single one of you. There is one really important part that only you can do Bill. Can you go and get Dave, Steve and Franky from the top of the skyscraper? We will need their help too."

"Of course," said Bill.

"I know those three well, it was Dave that told me where to find you, and Steve couldn't stop telling me stories about all the things you lot got up to."

"Franky will absolutely love this, it's a good chance to use that big old Pigeon brain of his."

Bill held out his wing to Blinky, and after getting some Plum, he flashed a smile and flapped off through the leaves. Bill soared up and off towards the distant tower.

Blinky turned to Aura. "I think this really could work you know, I hope the Pigeons are up for it too."

"I'm sure they will be Blinky, it sounds like they're good friends. Please tell me a little more about your adventures while we wait for them, if you don't mind?"

"Welllllllll," he started. "Tell me, what do you know about cookies?"

Chapter 18
The Plan

While Blinky was still describing to Aura, all of the different types, and tastes of cookies. Eric was telling the fascinated Spiderlings, about a nature documentary on Spiders he had seen. They were amazed to hear that Spiders came in so many different sizes and colours, and they loved learning about all the exotic places that they lived in.

Aura had never seen, let alone tasted a cookie before. But Blinkys detailed description was making her mouth water, and her tummy rumble.

They were interrupted by a familiar voice from above. "That's it. In there!" It was Bills distant but distinctive voice, and it was coming from just outside the canopy.

A moment later, three Pigeons came barging through the leaves one by one. It was Dave, then Steve, and last but by no means least, Franky.

All of the Pigeons were carrying a cookie in each hand, which always made landing a bit tricky. Even so, Franky still managed to pull off an impressive move as he came in to land.

The fact that six cookies were now on the scene, didn't go un-noticed by Eric. He couldn't contain himself at the sight of his favourite food, and came bounding excitedly out of the shadows, promptly launching himself straight at Franky.

Even though Bill had told the Pigeons about Eric, the huge tarantula surging towards them out of the darkness, was enough to make all of them scream out in terror.

Frankys instinctive reaction, was to fire one of his cookies straight at the lurching arachnid. It hit Eric square in the face, which made him screech to a stop with a loud. "OWWWWWW." Followed by, "Oooooh Hellooooo."

Eric did not waste any time, and began stuffing his face as fast as he could. So, it was left to Blinky to make the introductions. After Bill had also come in to land, and everyone had said hello. Blinky suggested that they go into the tree hollow, and discuss, "THE PLAN"

Blinky explained exactly what he wanted to do in the tree, offering the Pigeons a place to stash any excess food, safely. That way they wouldn't lose any goodies to the bins, and could come back for it the next day. There was only one charge for this service, that Eric could help himself.

"Sounds fair enough," said Dave. "There's always plenty going spare, and I'm sure the others on the rooftop will all agree."

Franky was acting a little out of character, he was unusually animated, and even looked ever so slightly excited.

He was already planning how best to make all this work. Quietly in his mind, he was coming up with ideas left, right, and centre.

"How about this Eric, if you weave a really strong web up near the top of the tree, we could use it as a drop off point. That way we can deliver packages on the wing, without having to wrestle them through the thick leaves?"

It was then that Eric, who had finally finished his cookie, got involved.

"I've seen a few building programmes on the television. They were a bit boring, but I couldn't be bothered to jump out my box to change the channel. I think, that with a bit of planning, we could make just the thing!"

"We need to check out a suitable location," Franky added. "I'll have a scout from above and look for a nice gap in the leaves. Eric if you could make your way up to the top of the trunk, I'll meet you there in ten minutes."

Eric nodded in agreement and started climbing, while Franky launched himself dramatically into a vertical take off. He had completely forgotten about the very light Spiderlings, who were blown off their feet, and up into the air by the powerful wing beats. The poor little things were splattered hard up against the trunk, ending up pinned firmly, with legs akimbo, at varying heights.

From that moment onward, Eric and Franky were inseparable! Erics' vast wealth of knowledge, combined with Frankys immeasurable brain power, was an extremely potent mix. It would soon become clear, that this unlikely partnership, would be a vital element to the success of this daunting building project.

While they were gone, the others discussed what possible options they might have for the main structure. Turning the big old tree into a permanent home for all of them, required quite some consideration.

Blinky took the lead in the discussion. "Eric told me that he recognised the leaves that cover this tree, from one of the documentaries he has watched. Apparently it is a deciduous tree, that means it will shed all of it's leaves in the Autumn. So one thing we must bear in mind, is how to keep it warm, and sheltered during the cold winter months.

Dave pointed out that the only real materials they consistently had at their disposal, was their own silk. He added, "Maybe you could weave so much silk, it would keep the wind, and rain out?"

As he said it, Franky spiralled down from above, with Eric bounding in not far behind.

"We've got it!" Franky said proudly. "We have found the perfect place for the drop off, Eric is an absolute gold mine of knowledge!"

"That's brilliant," said Blinky. "We do have one more challenge for you two to ponder over though."

He explained to the duo, the problems that the changing seasons presented, Franky suggested that they should go out onto the outer branches, to survey the area from a distance.

After a few minutes of thoughtfully looking around, and Franky occasionally put his wing to his beak while making a, "Hmmmmm," sound. He finally said, "I think your best bet, is to focus on strengthening around the tree hollow. There, you have a good solid sheltered structure to build out from, and some good strong branches to expand out on to."

Eric had been thinking exactly the same thing, and he had an important contribution to make. "The humans use something called insulation, its a kind of barrier that keeps the heat in, and the cold out. We need something like that."

Franky, inspired by Erics input said. "Yes, Yes... If we make a completely enclosed web structure, and added lots of layers around it, that should do the same job."

Always the one to point out the obvious, and just to be involved, Steve jumped in with. "That sounds like an awful lot of work, we would need masses upon masses of Silk. Even with all of you spinning non stop, it would still take ages. And remember, we only have what is left of the Summer to do it in."

"We need more spinners!" Stated Blinky. He turned to Aura, "Aura, what about the other weavers? The ones that left for the tall grasses, do you think they might be persuaded to come back?"

Aura thought for a moment. "I'm sure they would come back if they knew it was safe, but how are we going to get word to them? the grasses are a very long way from here!"

Blinky had a brain wave and turned to Bill. "What about you Bill, do you think you could find them, and tell them what's going on here?"

Aura interrupted, "They would never let him get close enough to talk to them! Even if he could, they would never trust the word of a bird."

Blinky thought hard for a moment, "I've got an idea! Bill, remember when you carried me on your back, over the road that day we met."

"Yes Blinky of course, but you're way to big for me to carry now."

"I know, but the Spiderlings aren't." He turned to the Spiderlings, who after peeling themselves off the trunk, were all again listening intensely, to the extraordinary debate that was unfolding around them.

Blinky spotted the bold little Spider, who was the first he had met in the tree.

"Spider, come to the front please. How would you like to earn your name today?"

Spider jumped to the front excitedly, "Definitely! What do you want me to do?"

"I need you to be very brave and ride on Bills back, he will carry you all the way to the grasslands. Your task there, is to convince as many of the weavers as you can, to come back here and help."

Little Spider looked up at Bill, who stretched out his wing like a ramp for Spider to climb up on. He gulped with uncertainty, and looked back at Blinky.

"You can do it," Blinky reassured. "We can't do this without your help!"

Spider took a deep breath and climbed gingerly up onto Bills back. "I will need to introduce myself when I get there though?" He looked to Blinky for the name he had promised him, the name he would be called for the rest of his life.

Blinky already knew exactly what that name would be.

"Well, seen as you will be the only other Spider here to have flown, and seen as I'm not using it anymore. I give you the name Kite!"

It was perfect!

Young Kite beamed with joy, but only for a second. Bill did his naughty trick of dropping sharply off the branch, everyone rushed eagerly to the edge to see where they had gone. But Bill and little Kite were already out of sight, all they could hear of them was young Kites' scream, as it slowly faded into the distance.

Chapter 19
Foundations

It had been decided, that the most crucial, and first part of the construction was to be the supporting silk. As it was this, that would hold the weight of all of the other interior web constructs.

By tapping into Erics vast knowledge in the field of construction, Franky managed to come up with an ingenious solution.

Because even with Erics very, very thick silk. It still might not be strong enough, to hold up the sheer weight of all of the buildings, never mind an ever growing colony of Spiders. Some more creative thinking was required!

Franky had the great idea, to twist three of Erics silk strands together. Like a, "Rope," as Eric had called it.

It was a stroke of pure genius, and further emphasised the potential of Eric and Frankys' combined minds.

This entwined super silk, made for an incredibly strong line. It was so strong, that even Dave could jump up and down on it with barely a bend, let alone any sign of breaking.

The combination of this strong silky rope, thorough planning, and huge effort from the two that would later become known, as the architects of the tree. Created a very sturdy framework, that completely encircled the trees hollow core.

Now, all it needed was the massive amount of silk required to join up the lattice of web rope. Thus completing, the inventive sphere within a sphere design, that gives it its strength. This was to become the foundation, that would make the web city in the tree completely protected. Not only insulating it from adverse weather conditions, but also giving a safe refuge, from any creatures that would want to cause them harm.

Eric was completely exhausted after spinning non stop for so many hours, it was lucky that there were two more cookies on hand to keep him going.

He needed both cookies, to replenish all the energy he had used weaving so much silk. As you may have guessed, nobody was going to argue with a hungry Eric. EVER!

While Eric and Franky busied themselves with the construction, Dave and Steve went back up to the rooftop, to tell all the other Pigeons about the amazing things, going on down in the big old Oak tree.

They eventually returned, fully loaded with as many tasty goodies as they could carry, which pleased Eric immensely.

Chapter 20
Reinforcements

It was not until late the next evening, Bill finally returned to the tree. He had little Kite riding majestically on his back, and it was pretty obvious from Kites face, that he had thoroughly enjoyed the ride. Just as much, if not more so than Blinky had done all those many months ago.

They brought very important news from the distant field full of weavers!

Bill swept along the long branch, which would soon become known as, "The runway!" Young Kite was holding tight to the soft feathers on the back of Bills neck. As they approached, Bill slightly flicked his wings vertically, causing him to decelerate rapidly. At the same time he dipped his head down, almost touching the branch below, young Kite let go of his feathered reigns, rolled over Bills head, down his beak, and landed perfectly on the branch.

"Ta Dahhhhhh!" "We're Back!" Shouted Kite, after his dramatic dismount.

Everyone cheered, applauded, and a couple even whooped, at the jaw dropping entrance.

But not Blinky! "How long have you been practising that?" He said looking at Bill disapprovingly.

Bill replied with a cheeky grin, "Once or twice, good though wasn't it?"

Bill quickly forgot he was being told off, and turned to take a bow to all the extremely impressed, and still clapping Spiderlings.

Blinky looked at Aura, who soon reigned her excited youngster in. "Kite, come here at once and tell us all what happened."

Young Kite snapped instinctively to his mothers command. "Yes mother," he called skipping over.

Now it was young Kite who had the stage. For the first time in his short life, he also felt the overwhelming pressure of having every ones eyes, only on him. Luckily he was a very confident young Spider, and a natural performer in public.

"Well everyone!" Kite stated boldly. He swept his front legs out to the entire audience, which immediately secured their undivided attention.

He started dramatically. "The journey was long, and fraught with many a peril!"

"We soared high, and we soared low. Out to the furthest edges of the park we journeyed." Kite was extremely animated in his descriptions, much to every ones enjoyment. He had a natural way of captivating the viewers, and much later on in his life, he would be the one to regail the tale to future generations.

Kite continued, "Me and Bill, we sailed over the vast expanse of the tall grasses. There we found big and elaborate webs, they were littered everywhere we looked. The colony was dispersed far and wide, so we had to start somewhere."

By this time, everyone had made themselves comfortable. They were all enjoying the adventure, as it unfolded from Kites little but loud lips.

"All were separated, scattered as far as the eye could see. So we had to make many, many stops. We approached each web, retelling the tale of the tree each time. That is how we got so good at making an entrance, it was a great way to get each Spider to at least talk to us."

"Are they coming?" Blinky interrupted.

Kite turned to him and said, "Some. Not all.

Most disappeared at the very sight of Bill, never to be seen again. Out of the ones brave enough to hear our tale, a lot of them were impossible to convince. They found it too hard to believe that such a feat was possible, deciding to stay in the safety of their deep grassy lairs instead."

Everyone sighed out loud in disappointment. What they didn't realise, was that Kite, being a natural story teller. Was just building the suspense, as he lead them to the positive climax of his story.

"However!" He said, stamping his feet to regain the audiences focus.

"There is, now as I speak. A decent sized group of the more adventurous of the adults, preparing to make the journey here. At this very moment, they are all grouping together and waiting for the cover of night, to make their way across the plains. To us!"

"How many?" Asked Blinky.

"At least twenty adult weavers," Kite replied, smiling.

At this point, Franky stepped forward. "That should be enough! With twenty adult weavers spinning day and night, we could have this place spun in less than a week!"

Everyone instantly erupted into cheer and applause, Kite was immediately the star of the tree.

Chapter 21
A Legend is born

That evening, there was a tangible positive buzz, all over the tree. Especially around the group of adults that were huddled together, as they excitedly discussed what would happen next.

It was decided that first, they would construct a huge insulated sphere. This would be their inner-most sanctuary, and the hub in which they could all come together, to discuss any issues that affected the colony.

Erics input on this democratic structure was invaluable, and it also made perfect sense to the others involved.

Then, they would weave the outer structures that would house all the inhabitants. It needed to be made in a way that could be easily expanded, as the population would definitely grow. It was truly, an idea of epic proportion!

As most of the Spiders settled down to sleep for the night, Dave and Steve returned to the rooftop, but Franky stayed behind with Eric. Frankys desire for knowledge was insatiable, and he was constantly drilling Eric for details on all kinds of things, especially aeronautics.

Eric had seen so many programmes about the flying machines that humans had made, this fascinated Franky beyond belief. For so long he had seen the steel birds that fly high above his head, now he had the chance to learn what they really were. He was amazed to find out, that there were actually humans inside them.

Nearly everybody was awake by the crack of dawn, they looked down over the park, all waiting for some sign of the new arrivals. Just after ten in the morning, Bill flew in excitedly announcing, that he had seen the group of bright Orb Weavers, they were approaching from the east.

Despite having already been spotted, and being so brightly coloured. The posse of weavers managed to go unseen, right up until they were at the very base of the tree.

They were clearly hesitant to climb the trunk now that they were there, they all knew of the Beast that stalks it's lower branches.

"Aura," Blinky called. "Why don't you go down and reassure them that it is safe, after all, they know you. I'll get Eric to hide for now, he will definitely need a gentle introduction."

So, after a little gentle persuasion from Aura, the group of 25 weavers, followed her up the trunk. They were warmly greeted, by the most unlikely group of friends they could ever have imagined.

The one who had fallen into the role of leader for their group, was called Driweave. Apparently she had pioneered a unique technique, that involved incorporating dry dead grasses directly into her web. This was something only she did, and this not only strengthened her webs, but also made them more camouflaged to the eyes of flies. This made her the most successful fly catcher on record, and she was also quite a large and very charismatic Spider.

After everyone had met and been shown around, there was just one thing left to do, introduce, Eric the Red!

Blinky stood up on a web platform, near the entrance to the tree hollow. After getting every ones attention, he went on to describe how they would all be protected from virtually any predator. This protection would be provided, by not only their friend, and wise advisor. But also the biggest, fiercest Spider that has ever lived.

"I give you, Eric the Red!"

Until then, Eric had been hiding within the tree hollow, planning his unveiling to the newcomers. He had squeezed himself into a tight gap, with his legs wedged in above his head like a coiled spring.

This is going to be hilarious, he thought to himself, as he eagerly awaited his cue from Blinky.

As Blinky said Red, Eric pushed himself up with all of his might. Nobody was expecting what happened next, not even Eric. He had drastically underestimated his own strength, and launched himself straight up and out the top of the tree hollow. He leapt with such force that he reached nearly a whole metre high, before gravity got the better of him.

All eyes followed the enormous Spider, as he rocketed out of the tree, wailing as he went.

"WAAAAAAAAAHHHHHHHHHHHHHHHHHHHHH, WEEEEEEEEEEEEEEEEEE, UH OH!"

Luckily he caught hold of one of his thick web ropes on the way down, and just dangled there for a moment. Everyone else stood frozen, staring at the unusual spectacle with mouths their mouths open.

Blinky shouted up, "You alright Eric?"

"Yep, yep, fine thanks." Came the reply, as he pulled himself up onto the support strand, and made his way back down to the branch.

At least any fear that the newcomers may have had, was now completely diffused, by the extraordinary entrance Eric had made. They were all still speechless as they watched the unbelievably massive Tarantula, descending back down towards them.

After a proper introduction, and the shock of Erics sheer size had passed. Eric explained how the support structure was put together, and what was needed next.

Driweave was instantly blown away, by the ingenious construction that Eric and Franky had put together. This really appealed to her forward way of thinking, and she was instantly recruited into Eric and Frankys team.

As Blinky, Eric, Franky and Driweave, started orchestrating where to start, beginning by delegating jobs to the other weavers. There was an unexpected series of flaps from above, followed by, "Bombs away... Look out below!"

It was a wing of Pigeons led by Dave, they were out on the day shift, and had obviously made a big find.

One by one, the Pigeons lined themselves up over the big, and super strong drop off web, this was its first real test. A human had dropped their entire breakfast on the floor, it was a fresh, saucy, sausage filled bap. Two Pigeons carried a piece of bread each, and one carried the sausage filling. It was quite a heavy load, so this would be a pretty substantial test of the webs resilience.

Driweave and the other newbies, hadn't yet been told about the arrangement with the Pigeons. So it was a bit of a shock, seeing an entire breakfast roll falling from the sky.

BOING, BOING, BOING. The three parts all landed safely in the middle of the web, bouncing slowly to a stop, in the seemingly unbreakable catch net.

"YESSSSS!" said Eric and Franky together, giving each other a high five.

Eric didn't stay to revel in its success for long, he knew exactly what had been delivered. He recognised the smell straight away and shot straight up the tree, heading directly for the sausage patty. This was his former owners favourite breakfast, and sometimes, if he was lucky, he got a piece thrown into his tank.

Driweave and the newbies had never tasted human food before, they were all a bit sceptical at first. That was, of course, until after they had their first taste of a choc chip cookie!

It was all working perfectly and the Pigeons came at least twice a day, laden with all kinds goodies.

Chapter 22
A new attraction

An effective system soon developed, and everyone had been assigned their tasks. Construction of the silk palace in the tree, was now well underway. Before long, the big main sphere was finished, and really was an impressive sight.

Blinky, having the up most confidence in the others, to start building the ancillary structures, turned his attention to the spheres interior. He decided to decorate the walls of the sphere, by spinning a 3d tapestry. He wanted to tell the story, of how this magnificent achievement had come to be. That way, even long after he was gone, the generations to come could see his story in silk.

Luckily, the thick shield of leaves concealed the increasingly large, and complex web structure from the outside. It went completely unnoticed by the humans. They would often pass by, totally unaware that they were just metres away, from the most extra-ordinary structure ever built in web.

Apart from the occasional Squirrel scurrying up the trunk, life was very peaceful in the tree of silk. Of course the cookie charged, ever ready Eric, was straight onto any intruders case.

Sometimes they escaped, never to return. Sometimes they didn't, and Eric being full up, left more cookies for the others for a couple of days.

By the time Autumns kiss, starting slowly eating away at the trees mass of leaves. Building work was well and truly complete.

The first human to notice it, was so startled that they dropped their lunch in shock and awe, this would later become Erics dinner of course.

After quite some commotion and debate among the humans, as to what it was, and what to do about it. They eventually decided, that this was a freak occurrence of nature, and should be preserved.

The tree of Silk soon became quite a popular attraction, people would come from far and wide, to look upon the massive city of silk. Nobody could quite figure out, what was going on hidden within its silk walls. Unable to see through the thick double web, they could only guess.

If only they knew!

The End

Eyes of The Fox

Written by

James Reece

Cover art by

Jasmin Koch

This story begins in the late afternoon,
of a stormy day with a rising full moon.

Young Denny's walking home, already late.
Unaware that this day was so laden with fate.

His day had been boring as usual so far.
And he did not like walking, he preferred the car.

But now here he was, getting urrrrgh, EXERCISE!
Of his life up till now, this was not one of the highs.

So down wooded path, he walked in a dream.
A normal day, or so it would seem.

Twigs break under foot, but wait... What's that sound?
He was certain nobody else was around.

There was an unnatural noise, from the bushes below.
It sounded quite near, fear started to grow!

A rustle, a bark, a growl then a scream.
Did a monster live there down by the stream?

Denny knew he should run as fast as he could,
but his legs were not working quite as they should.

On the spot he stood frozen, when in popped a thought.
What if the next person to come here gets caught?

He had to find out what this thing was for sure,
so he stepped up on the railing, so he could see more.

Too far over the fence he was leaning to peek,
when a loud crack of thunder followed bright
lightening streak.

With mud on his shoes Denny's grip was all gone.
Even with gloves, he could NOT hold on!

So down Denny tumbled without any doubt,
he was going to land with an almighty clout.

Ground and then trees were all that he saw.
A crash, a thud, and then nothing more.

The next thing he knew was the beautiful sound,
of rain bouncing off leaves before hitting the ground.

His vision came back but it was still such a blur,
all around him a swirl of bright orange fur!

One, two, three four foxes, or maybe more.
His vision was double so it was hard to be sure.

A whole family of foxes were stood all around,
one sitting so close it made his heart pound.

Its gaze was so focused, not even blinking.
The world all around him felt like it was shrinking.

Then in a flash they all darted away,
and all he could muster was a wobbly "HEY!"

Now Den was alone and the shower had passed,
soon it would be dark and he must get home fast.

His head was so sore when he got to the door,
how much he would say, he still was not sure.

Dennys' parents were worried, his mum was in tears.
She hugged him as though she had not seen him in
years.

He wolfed down his dinner and nothing was said,
about the four foxes before going to bed.

That night he slept deeply, tucked tight as he dreamed.
He dreamt of a place that was real, so it seemed.

Racing through woods by the light of the moon,
he had the strange feeling he would be home soon.

But this was not his house it was a hole in a bush,
yet through it he went with eyes shut and a push.

A tunnel he followed, all prickly and round,
what was this place that his dreamland had found?

It was absolute darkness 360 pitch black,
but Denny's other senses soon picked up the slack.

He felt safe in this place there was no sense of fear,
then his mum woke him up calling "Breakfast dear".

At school the next day on his dream he did dwell,
and boy did the bump on his head throb and swell.

Most times a dream is gone soon after you wake,
but this one stayed clear, well after lunch break.

That night Denny dreamt of the woods once more,
but this time it felt much more real than before.

The moonlight that broke through the trees to the ground,
Flickered in the breeze and danced all around.

In his dream Denny felt like he was close to the floor,
instead of standing upright he was down on all four.

He leant over a pool to have a quick drink,
but the reflection was not his it was, well what do
you think?

A young fox stared back up with his tongue hanging out,
and a little black nose at the end of its snout.

Through the eyes of the Fox young Denny could see,
through the dark of the night with such clarity

It was much more than that he could also feel,
How hungry Fox was, he needed a meal.

So they went off together and food was the quest,
Fox had to find dinner before he could rest.

The sky was ink black so it must have been late,
as the Fox squeezed himself under a gate.

Fox searched with all senses and then spotted a bin,
"that smells like there is something yummy within".

Up onto his hind and with the push of a paw,
the bin fell and emptied all over the floor.

Denny woke with a jolt as the bin hit the ground,
back in his bedroom, safe and sound.

What he saw the next morning made him stop in his track,
and even take a step or two back.

There stood an old man he was sweeping the floor,
clearing up all the mess made by fox he was sure.

Even though the drive was nearly all clean,
Denny was sure he recognised the scene.

He started to think he was going quite mad,
or it could be the knock to the head that he had.

There was only one person in which Den could confide,
Jim, his best friend was always on side.

He explained in great detail as he perched on a swing,
all the crazy things that had happened to him.

Jim listened intently to the story Den told,
about foxes in woods and passing out cold.

Jim thought for a while and then finally said,
"maybe that fox got into your head".

"There is only one way to know for sure,
let's see if tonight you dream of him more".

That night as before he was back in the wood,
at the edge of the trees the young fox and Den stood.

His attention was locked by a man on the hill,
as he forced something shiny in a cars window sill.

He looked up from the car and he checked all around,
then popped open the door without making a sound.

Just before the thief slipped into the car,
Denny saw on his cheek a long deep scar.

With the cars alarm wailing and bright flashing light,
a screech and some smoke he was off into the night.

Through the eyes of the fox Den could see a long way,
when a lady ran out Fox knew not to stay.

So off into the bush with incredible speed,
    went Fox on his nightly mission to feed.

It all seemed so real he could almost feel,
    the wind on his face as Fox bounced heel to heel.

The connection between them must be getting stronger,
    as the length of this dream was certainly longer.

Then up ahead sprung a faint light,
    poor Fox had not eaten since early last night.

Denny soon recognised it was Windrushes' Farm,
    Fox crept to it slowly not to break the nights calm.

His nose started to twitch at some delicious scent,
    too young and too hungry, all caution went.

Fox ran even quicker foot following nose,
    his belly rumbled as excitement rose.

Suddenly a door opened off to the right,
    Then the fox and Denny saw a terrible sight.

Racing toward them, clear leaping a log,
    was farmer Windrushes' enormous dog.

The fox changed direction but he turned way too fast,
    he couldn't keep one foot in front of the last.

He nearly went down in a heap on the floor,
    if he had there is no doubt Fox would be no more.

But with a flick of his tail and a cheeky foxtrot,
    back into the wood Fox and dreamer Den shot.

They didn't get far when an almighty SNAP!
  fox got his leg caught in a big metal trap.

Denny woke with a jolt grabbing his heel,
  he wasn't hurt but the pain felt so real.

He limped up to the window and looked out on the dawn,
  was there really a fox trapped out there this morn.

He closed his eyes and then in a flash,
  he was fox looking down at a terrible gash.

Save Fox now he must, if only he could.
  Get help to him all the way down in the wood.

Denny's mum wouldn't listen to his desperate plea,
  she was far too busy with her 3rd cup of tea.

She looked up at last and saw all of the sweat,
  "Denny your pyjamas," she cried, "You're all wet."

She dried him and dressed him then into the car,
  "We will go straight to the doctor, he doesn't live
    far."

Denny said to his mum "But mum I'm not sick,"
  I promise that this is not some kind of trick."

"It's the fox from my dreams he is in terrible danger!
  and I know what I'm saying could not sound any
    stranger."

His mum then replied "what fox is that dear?
  I think with this fever you're not thinking clear"

"Please take the back road that passes the wood?"
  "I'm sure I'd feel better if only we could."

She drove down the road Denny's dream had seen,
 but a police car was now parked where the other had
 been.

A policeman was standing outside the front door,
 it was the same door from the night before.

As they drove past the house Denny's window was down,
 he called out to a lady in her pink dressing gown.

"Excuse me but if someone has taken your car,
 all I saw of the thief was that his face had a scar."

The cop spun around and he shouted, "hey wait,"
 as he ran down the path to the front gate.

He looked hard at Denny "how could you know?
 such details of a crime only hours ago."

"There is a man at the station in our custody,
 who fits your description right down to a tee."

Denny explained what he'd seen while he was asleep,
 through the eyes of a fox from over the creek.

He told all of his story from beginning to end,
 then he pleaded if there was any help they could
 send.

"It is hard to believe but it is not a lie,
 if you can help me save fox I'm begging please try."

For a while there was silence and nobody spoke,
 slowly realising that all of this was not a joke.

Denny's mum was in shock and her jaw hung down low,
    what to make of all this she did not quite know.

"If you really did see all those things in the night,
    and were somehow connected to that foxes' sight."

"Then it stands to good reason that the ending is true,
    if you know where that fox is then I'll follow you."

Denny told them, "he is over on Windrushes land,
    but he's hurt really badly, can the vet lend a hand?"

The policeman then said, "There's no time to waste,
    if he's still in the trap then we must leave with
        haste."

They were there really fast with the vet on the way,
    Denny took them all straight to where the fox lay.

The trap was still clamped around Foxes' leg tight,
    you could tell from the bushes he had put up a fight.

But now he was still, no movement at all.
    Denny started to weep, then sob and then bawl.

The vet got there fast and looked at the fox,
    then she lifted him gently into a box.

"He is in a bad way but he is still alive,
    I will do what I can to help him survive."

No sign from the vet and two days had passed,
    then late that afternoon the phone rang at last.

With his leg set in plaster, some care and some time.
    Denny's new friend the Fox, would soon be fine.

Dens relief was so great that he made an odd noise,
  it was kind of a SQUEAL that's not normal for boys.

In a couple of weeks, the Fox would be free,
  and the vet asked if Denny would like to come see.

"I'd love to be there and I know just the place."
  He was so looking forward to seeing Foxes face.

As the time grew close Denny's excitement grew,
  would Fox be aware of the journey they had been
    through.

He already knew where to let the fox go,
  the safe den in the woods that his first dream did
    show.

So as once before Denny showed them the way,
  to the safe secret place where foxes did lay.

There was no sign from fox not even a sound,
  until the second that the box hit the ground.

He must have known that his home was near,
  and up until then been frozen with fear.

Denny whispered to Fox before he opened the door,
  "you are free now dear Fox we will stay friends I'm
    sure."

With a flick of the latch the young fox was freed,
  He struck out of the box with incredible speed.

You would not have known he had injured his paw,
  with the speed that the orange and white fluff ball
    tore.

Fox glanced back at Denny as if to show,
that all that had happened he also did know.

Denny smiled to himself at least once a day,
long after the dreams of Fox faded away.

The connection was lost, he could no longer be,
the fox in the woods as free as can be.

He did not feel sad but it was something he missed,
this point in his life with a magical twist.

Denny gazed down the garden one day deep in thought,
when a flash of bright orange fur his eye caught.

It was Fox! he had come! Denny leapt down the stair,
catching his dad completely unaware.

Before dad could conceal the extra pud he had taken,
Denny was out in the garden with a pack full of
bacon.

Just at that moment Mum entered the scene,
and glared at her husband licking his spoon clean.

Denny came back in with a smile ear to ear,
"that fox that I saved, he was just here"

She started to speak but stopped in her track,
upon seeing the empty smoked bacon pack.

"It looks like we have one more mouth to feed,
I will talk to the vet about what food we need."

Dad built Fox a shelter from old pallets he'd found,
so Fox could stay safe when he came around.

The fox always came every night without fail,
      then one summer night he saw more than one tail.

Four more tails he counted each white at the tip,
      All four with heads down fighting for the next sip.

The life the fox led was incredibly free,
      but he realised that this freedom carried with it a fee.

He learned that the fox got much pleasure from life,
      and that the joy of the moment was worth all the
           strife.

Be thankful if there's a roof over your head,
      fresh food in the fridge and a cosy warm bed.

The End

Printed in Great Britain
by Amazon